Collector's Library

JULIUS CAESAR

JULIUS CAESAR

William Shakespeare

INTRODUCTION BY
NED HALLEY

Collector's Library

Julius Caesar first published 1600
This edition published in 2013 by
Collector's Library
an imprint of CRW Publishing Limited,
69 Gloucester Crescent, London NW1 7EG

ISBN 978 1 907360 82 4

2 4 6 8 10 9 7 5 3 1

Typeset in Great Britain by
Bookcraft Ltd, Stroud, Gloucestershire

Printed and bound in China by Imago

Contents

Introduction

Julius Caesar was murdered at a theatre in the city of Rome on the morning of 15 March in the year 44BC. He was 55, dictator of Rome, and the most powerful individual in the western world. His assassination triggered a series of civil wars that destroyed the Republic, the constitutional system of government that had displaced the Roman monarchy 450 years previously.

Under the Republic, Rome was ruled by consuls, elected for just one year at a time. To begin with they were all aristocrats, the patricians, but in later centuries faced rivalry from a new, aspiring, self-made class, the plebeians. Power became divided between these two factions, but in common they shared a deep sense of public duty. The Republic, politically and ethically stable, prospered from imperialism, occupying all of southern Europe, tracts of northern Africa and Asia and latterly parts of northern Europe, including Britain.

Caesar was a patrician from an ancient landed dynasty, the Julii. A military commander before he was 21, a famous incident showed his character. Kidnapped by pirates, he promised he would pay a ransom, and that on his release he would return and crucify all of them. They thought it was bravado, but he kept his word in every respect. Caesar rose rapidly through the political ranks as a heroic public figure and in 60BC formed the first triumvirate of Roman rulers with Pompey, a general second only to Caesar in reputation, and Crassus, the richest man in Rome. It was an unofficial, largely secret, alliance but wielded great power, rivalling even that of the Republic's legislative body, the senate. In 59 Caesar was elected consul.

Between 58 and 50 while Caesar was on military duty, Crassus was killed in battle in Asia. Pompey began to seek his own power base in Rome. Finally, on learning that Caesar was in Cisalpine Gaul (now northern Italy) intending to march on Rome with his victorious legions, Pompey had the senate order him to quit his command and disband his armies. Caesar refused, crossed the Rubicon river into Italy (it was treason to enter the country under arms) and defeated Pompey in a civil war that ranged across Italy and elsewhere in the empire. Pompey fled to Egypt where he was murdered, and Caesar was appointed both consul and dictator. Even then, he marched to Egypt (in 47) to enforce the rule of his mistress, Cleopatra, and finally defeated the last of Pompey's armies in Africa and Spain.

When Caesar returned to Rome in 45, the senate, further cowed by his triumphs, reappointed him consul for ten years, dictator in perpetuity, and 'Father of the Nation'. Statues of him were placed in the temples of the city and his profile minted on to the coinage. Caesar had become a demi-god.

This is where we find him at the outset of Shakespeare's play. Formally entitled *The Tragedy of Julius Caesar*, it was written probably in 1599, and based on the 1579 translation by Sir Thomas North of two biographies by Plutarch, the Greek historian and philosopher (45–120 AD), *The Life of Brutus* and *The Life of Caesar*. Known to scholarship as the encyclopaedist of antiquity, a great amount of Plutarch's work has survived, and his accuracy as a reporter has been corroborated by the work of contemporaries such as Suetonius, author of *The Lives of the Caesars*.

Shakespeare's version of this pivotal event in world history has reliable provenance. The *dramatis personae* are all drawn from history. The famous oddities of the play, the anachronistic references to a striking clock (a late-medieval invention) and to Elizabethan-style attire such as hats and doublets, have been attributed to the notion that the play makes veiled reference to the question of the royal succession. In 1599 Queen Elizabeth was old and ailing, and had not named an heir. There was consequently some alarm that there could be civil war after her death, as there had been after Caesar's.

JULIUS CAESAR

The principal purpose of *Julius Caesar* is more obvious. The playwright exploits the episode to deliver a powerful exposition on ambition, friendship and betrayal. Caesar was certainly the most ambitious of men. His achievements to date, and his plans for the future, including a comprehensive reform of Roman law, vast infrastructure projects and foreign adventures, were feared by the leading Romans of his day as well as admired. And Caesar's ambitions for himself were an understandable matter for speculation. Did he desire the restoration of the Roman monarchy, with himself the first king back on the throne since Tarquin, the sixth successor to founding sovereign Romulus, who had been, at least according to legend, unseated in 509BC?

We will never know whether Caesar's ambition extended this far, but the possibility of it is certainly what cost him his life. And he made himself more vulnerable through his mercy. Most unusually for a Roman general, Caesar had the characteristic of showing *clementia* – clemency – to his defeated enemies. This was as true in civil conflict as it was in wars of invasion, and it had been extended to the two principal conspirators against his life, both in fact and as portrayed in the play. Brutus had sided with Pompey in the civil war of 49, but submitted to Caesar after the defeat, and was rewarded with the governorship of Cisalpine Gaul. Cassius had been a quaestor, a treasury official, in the service of Crassus until the triumvir's death. Like Brutus, Cassius had taken Pompey's side in the civil war. Caesar had pardoned him and advanced his political career.

In the opening scene of the play, it is a public holiday, Lupercalia (15 February), and two tribunes (elected officials similar to police) accost a couple of workmen on their way to join the crowd welcoming Caesar's triumphant entry into Rome. The tribunes personify the old regime, telling the men that Caesar brings with him nothing of the spoils and glory that Pompey once did:

> O you hard hearts, you cruel men of Rome,
> Knew you not Pompey? Many a time and oft

Have you climb'd up to walls and battlements,
To towers and windows, yea, to chimney tops,
Your infants in your arms, and there have sat
The livelong day with patient expectation
To see great Pompey pass the streets of Rome.

Pompey, though dead four years, still embodies the resistance to the irresistible Caesar. But the opposition, as manifested in chief conspirators Cassius and Brutus in Act I Scene II, is at best equivocal. The audience might not know, though Shakespeare surely did, that these two senior politicians owed not just their elevated status but their very lives to Caesar. This does not deter Cassius from turning Brutus against their benefactor, on the unsubstantiated apprehension that Caesar wishes for a crown. Brutus is taken in. Hearing the crowd call out for Caesar, he surmises Cassius must be right about the dictator's ambition.

Brutus
What means this shouting? I do fear the people
Choose Caesar for their king.

Cassius
Ay, do you fear it?
Then must I think you would not have it so.

Brutus
I would not, Cassius, yet I love him well.

Caesar has as much to fear from his friends as he has ever done from his enemies. And in the best traditions of classical tragedy, he ignores or misses the warnings that he should stay at home on the fateful day. He makes light of Cassius's suspicious demeanour in the famous phrase 'he has a lean and hungry look' and dismisses as 'a dreamer' the soothsayer who warns him, to his face, to beware the ides of March. Even his wife Calpurnia's graphically related dreams and premonitions of his murder are put aside, as is the advice of the priests, whose sacrifice augurs ill. Only briefly does Calpurnia's plea to Caesar on her knees persuade him to consider sending the trusted soldier Mark Antony to say he is unwell, but in the final twist, conspirator Decius Brutus plays the ace card. The senate, he warns, might put its leader's absence down to foolishness, or even fear. Decius deploys a whole battery of emotional blackmail, including flattery, mockery and protestations of his own love for the intended victim in order to seal his fate.

> And know it now, the Senate have concluded
> To give this day a crown to mighty Caesar.
> If you shall send them word you will not come,
> Their minds may change. Besides, it were a mock
> Apt to be render'd, for someone to say
> 'Break up the Senate till another time,
> When Caesar's wife shall meet with better dreams.'
> If Caesar hide himself, shall they not whisper
> 'Lo, Caesar is afraid'?
> Pardon me, Caesar, for my dear dear love
> To your proceeding bids me tell you this,
> And reason to my love is liable.

Caesar calls for his robe. He will go. Who would do otherwise? The scene is an exceptionally tense one of dénouement towards the tragic outcome, and building too on the mighty dictator's fatal flaw of believing in his own infallibility. He is immediately swept up in the gaggle of conspirators for the short journey to the Capitol.

In setting the crime at the Capitol, seat of the senate, Shakespeare makes a diversion from the historic event. According to Plutarch, Caesar was killed at the Theatre of Pompey, at the time the principal place of entertainment in the city, which doubled as a venue for public meetings. Given the significance of Pompey's legacy in the events themselves, and in the play, it might seem a curious departure, but the Capitol was in fairness the most important building of any kind in Rome. Note that the Theatre of Flavius, later known as the Colosseum, Rome's largest amphitheatre, was not built until the latter part of the following century.

Just as the tension of Caesar's progress to the wrong decision is so skilfully wrought in Act II, so is the arrival at a fatal error of judgment made by the conspirators. It is to spare Mark Antony. Cassius wants him killed with Caesar – 'it is not meet/Mark Antony, so well beloved of Caesar/Should outlive Caesar' – but Brutus balks at it:

> Our course will seem too bloody, Caius Cassius,
> To cut the head off and then hack the limbs
> Like wrath in death and envy afterwards;
> For Antony is but a limb of Caesar.
> Let us be sacrificers, but not butchers, Caius.

Brutus has been persuaded against his better nature to join the conspiracy, but his motive is, he believes, honourable. He will not countenance what appears to be the gratuitous crime of killing Mark Antony as well. Cassius's fatal mistake is to concede. Mark Antony, we know, will be their undoing. It is not their crime of murder that will condemn them, it is their clemency.

And so, in Act III Scene I, just half way through the play, the action of the assassination takes place. Brutus strikes the final blow, Caesar utters the anticipated line 'Et tu, Brute?' – And you, Brutus? – and the deed is done. This is a further departure from Plutarch, who relates that the victim said nothing when he was attacked, but there was a very much more recent precedent for the phrase; it was already a stock line in earlier sixteenth-century dramatizations of the murder.

The portentous orations over the body that follow are, however, entirely of Shakespeare's imagining. Again, Cassius is wary of Mark Antony. He warns Brutus in advance not to allow him to speak at the funeral, but again Brutus fails to take his advice, trusting Mark Antony 'shall not in your funeral speech blame us.'

In this section of the play, Shakespeare compresses the historic events. In Act III Scenes I and II, Caesar is murdered, his funeral held and will published all within hours. In Plutarch, while the murder took place on 15 March, the will was not made public until 18 March and the funeral was conducted on 20 March. And the arrival of Octavius (Octavian, Caesar's adopted son and the future first Roman emperor, Augustus) shortly after in Act IV is brought forward a full two months of the date of his actual entry into Rome, on 20 May. The formation of the Second Triumverate between Mark Antony, Octavian and Lepidus (former consul and loyalist of Caesar) which appears to take place immediately after Caesar's funeral is brought even further forward, and set in Rome instead of in its historic location, Bolonia in Cisalpine Gaul, late in 43BC. The two battles of Philippi (in Macedonia) between the Triumverate and the conspirators that Shakespeare contracts into a single rout concluded the widespread civil wars that followed the assassination, in October 42.

Shakespeare's purpose is to imagine the human feelings arising from such great historic events, and the first of these feelings is the rage, left unexpressed until Mark Antony is left alone by the conspirators, whom he understandably feared might kill him, but for Brutus's protection. Standing over the body of Caesar, Mark Antony invokes the Greek deity Ate, goddess of vengeance, in his rage against the crime:

> And Caesar's spirit ranging for revenge,
> With Ate by his side come hot from hell,
> Shall in these confines with a monarch's voice
> Cry 'Havoc!' and let slip the dogs of war,
> That this foul deed shall smell above the earth
> With carrion men, groaning for burial.

But in Act III Scene II before the throng in the Forum, Caesar's champion seems to strike a conciliatory note in his reply to Brutus's funeral speech defending the crime on the grounds 'not that I love Caesar less, but that I loved Rome more' and that 'As Caesar loved me, I weep for him; as he was fortunate, I rejoice at it; as he was valiant, I honour him; but as he was ambitious, I slew him.'

The crowd is persuaded that Brutus acted for Rome, and when Mark Antony takes his turn at the rostrum he seems at first to agree. Brutus, he says, believed Caesar was ambitious, but ambitious for Caesar more than for Rome. It sounds plausible. But what of Brutus? Where does his ambition lie? Mark Antony's address to his 'Friends, Romans, countrymen' inserts the knife into Brutus (who has by now departed the Forum) with the same certainty of mortal wounding as the conspirators' daggers have done.

> The noble Brutus
> Hath told you Caesar was ambitious;
> If it were so, it was a grievous fault,
> And grievously hath Caesar answer'd it.
> Here, under leave of Brutus and the rest –
> For Brutus is an honourable man;
> So are they all, all honourable men –
> Come I to speak in Caesar's funeral.
> He was my friend, faithful and just to me;
> But Brutus says he was ambitious,
> And Brutus is an honourable man.

Ambition and honour are at the heart of this great play. They are the very instincts that created and maintained the Roman Republic, perhaps the greatest political endeavour in history, and now they are shown to be the instruments of its destruction. Shakespeare manifests this dichotomy in beautiful language, and in a piquant reminder of the perils of power. And he tempers the morality tale with an unexpected twist of forgiveness – the first among human virtues – at the close of the play. Learning of Brutus's suicide, Mark Antony pays this tribute:

> This was the noblest Roman of them all.
> All the conspirators, save only he,
> Did that they did in envy of great Caesar;
> He only, in a general honest thought
> And common good to all, made one of them.

JULIUS CAESAR

His life was gentle, and the elements
So mix'd in him that Nature might stand up
And say to all the world, 'This was a man!'

JULIUS CAESAR

DRAMATIS PERSONAE

JULIUS CAESAR.
OCTAVIUS CAESAR,
MARCUS ANTONIUS, } *triumvirs after the death of Julius Caesar*

M. AEMILIUS LEPIDUS,
CICERO, } *senators*
PUBLIUS,

POPILIUS LENA,
MARCUS BRUTUS,
CASSIUS,
CASCA,
TREBONIUS, } *conspirators against Julius Caesar*
LIGARIUS,
DECIUS BRUTUS,
METELLUS CIMBER,

CINNA, *conspirator against Julius Cæsar.*
FLAVIUS *and* MARULLUS, *tribunes.*
ARTEMIDORUS, *a sophist of Cnidos.*
A SOOTHSAYER.
CINNA, *a poet.*
ANOTHER POET.

LUCILIUS,
TITINIUS,
MESSALA, } *friends to Brutus and Cassius*
YOUNG CATO,
VOLUMNIUS,

VARRO,
CLITUS,
CLAUDIUS,
STRATO, } *servants to Brutus*
LUCIUS,
DARDANIUS,

PINDARUS, *servant to Cassius.*
CALPHURNIA, *wife to Cæsar.*
PORTIA, *wife to* BRUTUS.
SENATORS, CITIZENS, GUARDS, ATTENDANTS, *etc.*

SCENE — *During a great part of the play at Rome; afterwards near Sardis, and near Philippi.*

ACT I

SCENE I

Rome. A street.

Enter FLAVIUS, MARULLUS,
and a rabble of CITIZENS.

FLAVIUS

Hence! home, you idle creatures, get you home:
Is this a holiday? what! know you not,
Being mechanical, you ought not walk
Upon a labouring day without the sign
Of your profession? — Speak, what trade art thou?

FIRST CITIZEN

Why, sir, a carpenter.

MARULLUS

Where is thy leather apron and thy rule?
What dost thou with thy best apparel on? —
You, sir, what trade are you?

SECOND CITIZEN

Truly, sir, in respect of a fine workman, I am but, as you
would say, a cobbler.

MARULLUS

But what trade art thou? answer me directly.

SECOND CITIZEN

A trade, sir, that I hope I may use with a safe conscience;
which is, indeed, sir, a mender of bad soles.

MARULLUS

What trade, thou knave? thou naughty knave, what
trade?

SECOND CITIZEN

Nay, I beseech you, sir, be not out with me: yet if you be out, sir, I can mend you.

MARULLUS

What meanest thou by that? mend me, thou saucy fellow!

SECOND CITIZEN

Why, sir, cobble you.

FLAVIUS

Thou art a cobbler, art thou?

SECOND CITIZEN

Truly, sir, all that I live by is with the awl: I meddle with no tradesman's matters, nor women's matters, but with awl. I am, indeed, sir, a surgeon to old shoes; when they are in great danger, I recover them. As proper men as ever trod upon neats-leather have gone upon my handiwork.

FLAVIUS

But wherefore art not in thy shop to-day?
Why dost thou lead these men about the streets?

SECOND CITIZEN

Truly, sir, to wear out their shoes, to get myself into more work. But, indeed, sir, we make holiday, to see Cæsar, and to rejoice in his triumph.

MARULLUS

Wherefore rejoice? What conquest brings he home?
What tributaries follow him to Rome,
To grace in captive bonds his chariot-wheels?
You blocks, you stones, you worse than senseless things!
O you hard hearts, you cruel men of Rome,
Knew you not Pompey? Many a time and oft
Have you climb'd up to walls and battlements,
To towers and windows, yea, to chimney-tops,
Your infants in your arms, and there have sat
The live-long day, with patient expectation,
To see great Pompey pass the streets of Rome:

And when you saw his chariot but appear,
Have you not made an universal shout,
That Tiber trembled underneath her banks,
To hear the replication of your sounds
Made in her concave shores?
And do you now put on your best attire?
And do you now cull out a holiday?
And do you now strew flowers in his way
That comes in triumph over Pompey's blood?
Be gone!
Run to your houses, fall upon your knees,
Pray to the gods to intermit the plague
That needs must light on this ingratitude.

FLAVIUS

Go, go, good countrymen, and, for this fault,
Assemble all the poor men of your sort;
Draw them to Tiber banks, and weep your tears
Into the channel, till the lowest stream
Do kiss the most exalted shores of all.

[*Exeunt* CITIZENS.

See, whe'r their basest metal be not mov'd!
They vanish tongue-tied in their guiltiness.
Go you down that way towards the Capitol;
This way will I: disrobe the images,
If you do find them deck'd with ceremonies.

MARULLUS

May we do so?
You know it is the feast of Lupercal.

FLAVIUS

It is no matter; let no images
Be hung with Cæsar's trophies. I'll about,
And drive away the vulgar from the streets:
So do you too, where you perceive them thick.
These growing feathers pluck'd from Cæsar's wing
Will make him fly an ordinary pitch;
Who else would soar above the view of men,
And keep us all in servile fearfulness.

[*Exeunt.*

SCENE II

The same. A public place.

Enter in procession CAESAR; ANTONY, *for the course;*
CALPHURNIA, PORTIA, DECIUS, CICERO,
BRUTUS, CASSIUS, *and* ASCA; *a great crowd following,
among them a* SOOTHSAYER.

CAESAR
Calphurnia, —

CASCA
Peace, ho! Cæsar speaks.

                                             [Music ceases.

CAESAR
                   Calphurnia, —

CALPHURNIA
Here, my lord.

CAESAR
Stand you directly in Antonius' way,
When he doth run his course. — Antonius, —

ANTONY
Cæsar, my lord?

CAESAR
Forget not, in your speed, Antonius,
To touch Calphurnia; for our elders say,
The barren, touched in this holy chase,
Shake off their sterile curse.

ANTONY
                  I shall remember:
When Cæsar says 'Do this,' it is perform'd.

CAESAR
Set on; and leave no ceremony out.

                                               [Music.

SOOTHSAYER
Cæsar!

CAESAR
Ha! who calls?

CASCA

Bid every noise be still: — peace yet again!

[*Music ceases.*

CAESAR

Who is it in the press that calls on me?
I hear a tongue, shriller than all the music,
Cry 'Cæsar.' Speak; Cæsar is turn'd to hear.

SOOTHSAYER

Beware the ides of March.

CAESAR

What man is that?

BRUTUS

A soothsayer bids you beware the ides of March.

CAESAR

Set him before me; let me see his face.

CASSIUS

Fellow, come from the throng; look upon Cæsar.

CAESAR

What say'st thou to me now? speak once again.

SOOTHSAYER

Beware the ides of March.

CAESAR

He is a dreamer; let us leave him: — pass.

[*Sennet. Exeunt all but* BRUTUS *and* CASSIUS.

CASSIUS

Will you go see the order of the course?

BRUTUS

Not I.

CASSIUS

I pray you, do.

BRUTUS

I am not gamesome: I do lack some part
Of that quick spirit that is in Antony.
Let me not hinder, Cassius, your desires;
I'll leave you.

CASSIUS

Brutus, I do observe you now of late:
I have not from your eyes that gentleness
And show of love as I was wont to have:
You bear too stubborn and too strange a hand
Over your friend that loves you.

BRUTUS

Cassius,
Be not deceived: if I have veil'd my look,
I turn the trouble of my countenance
Merely upon myself. Vexed I am,
Of late, with passions of some difference,
Conceptions only proper to myself,
Which give some soil, perhaps, to my behaviours;
But let not therefore my good friends be griev'd, —
Among which number, Cassius, be you one, —
Nor construe any further my neglect,
Than that poor Brutus, with himself at war,
Forgets the shows of love to other men.

CASSIUS

Then, Brutus, I have much mistook your passion;
By means whereof this breast of mine hath buried
Thoughts of great value, worthy cogitations.
Tell me, good Brutus, can you see your face?

BRUTUS

No, Cassius; for the eye sees not itself
But by reflection from some other thing.

CASSIUS

'Tis just:
And it is very much lamented, Brutus,
That you have no such mirrors as will turn
Your hidden worthiness into your eye,
That you might see your shadow. I have heard,
Where many of the best respect in Rome, —
Except immortal Cæsar, — speaking of Brutus,
And groaning underneath this age's yoke,
Have wish'd that noble Brutus had his eyes.

BRUTUS

Into what dangers would you lead me, Cassius,
That you would have me seek into myself
For that which is not in me?

CASSIUS

Therefore, good Brutus, be prepared to hear:
And, since you know you cannot see yourself
So well as by reflection, I, your glass,
Will modestly discover to yourself
That of yourself which you yet know not of.
And be not jealous on me, gentle Brutus:
Were I a common laughter, or did use
To stale with ordinary oaths my love
To every new protester; if you know
That I do fawn on men, and hug them hard,
And after scandal them; or if you know
That I profess myself in banqueting
To all the rout, then hold me dangerous.

[*Flourish and shout.*

BRUTUS

What means this shouting? I do fear, the people
Choose Cæsar for their king.

CASSIUS

                    Ay, do you fear it?
Then must I think you would not have it so.

BRUTUS

I would not, Cassius; yet I love him well. —
But wherefore do you hold me here so long?
What is it that you would impart to me?
If it be aught toward the general good,
Set honour in one eye, and death i'th'other,
And I will look on both indifferently;
For, let the gods so speed me as I love
The name of honour more than I fear death.

CASSIUS

I know that virtue to be in you, Brutus,
As well as I do know your outward favour.

Well, honour is the subject of my story. —
I cannot tell what you and other men
Think of this life; but, for my single self,
I had as lief not be as live to be
In awe of such a thing as I myself.
I was born free as Cæsar; so were you:
We both have fed as well; and we can both
Endure the winter's cold as well as he:
For once, upon a raw and gusty day,
The troubled Tiber chafing with her shores,
Cæsar said to me, 'Darest thou, Cassius, now
Leap in with me into this angry flood,
And swim to yonder point?' Upon the word,
Accoutred as I was, I plunged in,
And bade him follow: so, indeed, he did.
The torrent roar'd; and we did buffet it
With lusty sinews, throwing it aside
And stemming it with hearts of controversy:
But ere we could arrive the point proposed,
Cæsar cried, 'Help me, Cassius, or I sink!'
I, as Aeneas, our great ancestor,
Did from the flames of Troy upon his shoulder
The old Anchises bear, so from the waves of Tiber
Did I the tired Cæsar: and this man
Is now become a god; and Cassius is
A wretched creature, and must bend his body,
If Cæsar carelessly but nod on him.
He had a fever when he was in Spain,
And, when the fit was on him, I did mark
How he did shake: 'tis true, this god did shake:
His coward lips did from their colour fly;
And that same eye, whose bend doth awe the world,
Did lose his lustre: I did hear him groan:
Ay, and that tongue of his, that bade the Romans
Mark him, and write his speeches in their books,
Alas, it cried, 'Give me some drink, Titinius,'
As a sick girl. Ye gods, it doth amaze me,

A man of such a feeble temper should
So get the start of the majestic world,
And bear the palm alone.

[*Flourish and shout.*

BRUTUS

Another general shout!
I do believe that these applauses are
For some new honours that are heap'd on Cæsar.

CASSIUS

Why, man, he doth bestride the narrow world
Like a Colossus; and we petty men
Walk under his huge legs, and peep about
To find ourselves dishonourable graves.
Men at some time are masters of their fates:
The fault, dear Brutus, is not in our stars,
But in ourselves, that we are underlings.
Brutus, and Cæsar: what should be in that Cæsar?
Why should that name be sounded more than yours?
Write them together, yours is as fair a name;
Sound them, it doth become the mouth as well;
Weigh them, it is as heavy; conjure with 'em,
Brutus will start a spirit as soon as Cæsar.
Now, in the names of all the gods at once,
Upon what meat doth this our Cæsar feed,
That he is grown so great? Age, thou art shamed!
Rome, thou hast lost the breed of noble bloods!
When went there by an age, since the great flood,
But it was fam'd with more than with one man?
When could they say, till now, that talk'd of Rome,
That her wide walls encompass'd but one man?
Now is it Rome indeed, and room enough,
When there is in it but one only man.
O, you and I have heard our fathers say,
There was a Brutus once that would have brook'd
Th'eternal devil to keep his state in Rome
As easily as a king.

BRUTUS

That you do love me, I am nothing jealous;
What you would work me to, I have some aim:
How I have thought of this, and of these times,
I shall recount hereafter; for this present,
I would not, so with love I might entreat you,
Be any further mov'd. What you have said,
I will consider; what you have to say,
I will with patience hear; and find a time
Both meet to hear and answer such high things.
Till then, my noble friend, chew upon this;
Brutus had rather be a villager
Than to repute himself a son of Rome
Under these hard conditions as this time
Is like to lay upon us.

CASSIUS

               I am glad
That my weak words have struck but this much show
Of fire from Brutus.

BRUTUS

The games are done, and Cæsar is returning.

CASSIUS

As they pass by, pluck Casca by the sleeve;
And he will, after his sour fashion, tell you
What hath proceeded worthy note to-day.

        Enter CAESAR *and his* TRAIN.

BRUTUS

I will do so: — but, look you, Cassius,
The angry spot doth glow on Cæsar's brow,
And all the rest look like a chidden train:
Calphurnia's cheek is pale; and Cicero
Looks with such ferret and such fiery eyes
As we have seen him in the Capitol,
Being cross'd in conference by some senator.

CASSIUS

Casca will tell us what the matter is.

CAESAR

Antonius, —

ANTONY

Cæsar?

CAESAR

Let me have men about me that are fat;
Sleek-headed men, and such as sleep o' nights:
Yond Cassius has a lean and hungry look;
He thinks too much: such men are dangerous.

ANTONY

Fear him not, Cæsar; he's not dangerous;
He is a noble Roman, and well given.

CAESAR

Would he were fatter! — but I fear him not;
Yet if my name were liable to fear,
I do not know the man I should avoid
So soon as that spare Cassius. He reads much;
He is a great observer, and he looks
Quite through the deeds of men: he loves no plays,
As thou dost, Antony; he hears no music;
Seldom he smiles; and smiles in such a sort
As if he mock'd himself, and scorn'd his spirit
That could be mov'd to smile at any thing.
Such men as he be never at heart's ease
Whiles they behold a greater than themselves;
And therefore are they very dangerous.
I rather tell thee what is to be fear'd
Than what I fear, — for always I am Cæsar.
Come on my right hand, for this ear is deaf,
And tell me truly what thou think'st of him.

      [*Exeunt* CAESAR *and all his* TRAIN *but* CASCA.

CASCA

You pull'd me by the cloak; would you speak with me?

BRUTUS

Ay, Casca; tell us what hath chanc'd to-day,
That Cæsar looks so sad.

CASCA You pull'd me by the cloak; would you speak with me?

CASCA
Why, you were with him, were you not?

BRUTUS
I should not, then, ask Casca what had chanc'd.

CASCA
Why, there was a crown offer'd him; and being offer'd
him, he put it by with the back of his hand, thus; and
then the people fell a-shouting.

BRUTUS
What was the second noise for?

CASCA
Why, for that too.

CASSIUS
They shouted thrice: what was the last cry for?

CASCA
Why, for that too.

BRUTUS
Was the crown offer'd him thrice?

CASCA

Ay, marry, was't, and he put it by thrice, every time
gentler than other; and at every putting-by mine honest
neighbours shouted.

CASSIUS

Who offer'd him the crown?

CASCA

Why, Antony.

BRUTUS

Tell us the manner of it, gentle Casca.

CASCA

I can as well be hang'd as tell the manner of it: it was
mere foolery; I did not mark it. I saw Mark Antony offer
him a crown; — yet 'twas not a crown neither, 'twas one
of these coronets; — and, as I told you, he put it by
once: but, for all that, to my thinking, he would fain
have had it. Then he offer'd it to him again; then he put
it by again: but, to my thinking, he was very loth to lay
his fingers off it. And then he offer'd it the third time; he
put it the third time by; and still as he refused it, the
rabblement shouted, and clapp'd their chopp'd hands,
and threw up their sweaty nightcaps, and utter'd such a
deal of stinking breath because Cæsar refused the
crown, that it had almost choked Cæsar; for he
swounded, and fell down at it: and for my own part, I
durst not laugh, for fear of opening my lips and
receiving the bad air.

CASSIUS

But, soft, I pray you: what, did Cæsar swound?

CASCA

He fell down in the market-place, and foam'd at mouth,
and was speechless.

BRUTUS

'Tis very like he hath the falling-sickness.

CASSIUS

No, Cæsar hath it not: but you, and I,
And honest Casca, we have the falling-sickness.

CASCA

I know not what you mean by that; but, I am sure,
Cæsar fell down. If the tag-rag people did not clap him
and hiss him, according as he pleased and displeased
them, as they use to do the players in the theatre, I am
no true man.

BRUTUS

What said he when he came unto himself?

CASCA

Marry, before he fell down, when he perceived the
common herd was glad he refused the crown, he pluck'd
me ope his doublet, and offer'd them his throat to cut:
— an I had been a man of any occupation, if I would
not have taken him at a word, I would I might go to hell
among the rogues: — and so he fell. When he came to
himself again, he said, if he had done or said any thing
amiss, he desired their worships to think it was his
infirmity. Three or four wenches, where I stood, cried,
'Alas, good soul!' and forgave him with all their hearts:
but there's no heed to be taken of them; if Cæsar had
stabb'd their mothers, they would have done no less.

BRUTUS

And after that, he came, thus sad, away?

CASCA

Ay.

CASSIUS

Did Cicero say any thing?

CASCA

Ay, he spoke Greek.

CASSIUS

To what effect?

CASCA

Nay, an I tell you that, I'll ne'er look you i'th'face again:
but those that understood him smiled at one another,
and shook their heads; but, for mine own part, it was
Greek to me. I could tell you more news too: Marullus
and Flavius, for pulling scarfs off Cæsar's images, are

put to silence. Fare you well. There was more foolery
yet, if I could remember it.

CASSIUS

Will you sup with me to-night, Casca?

CASCA

No, I am promised forth.

CASSIUS

Will you dine with me to-morrow?

CASCA

Ay, if I be alive, and your mind hold, and your dinner
worth the eating.

CASSIUS

Good; I will expect you.

CASCA

Do so: farewell, both.

[*Exit.*

BRUTUS

What a blunt fellow is this grown to be!
He was quick mettle when he went to school.

CASSIUS

So is he now, in execution
Of any bold or noble enterprise,
However he puts on this tardy form.
This rudeness is a sauce to his good wit,
Which gives men stomach to digest his words
With better appetite.

BRUTUS

And so it is. For this time I will leave you:
To-morrow, if you please to speak with me,
I will come home to you; or, if you will,
Come home to me, and I will wait for you.

CASSIUS

I will do so: — till then, think of the world.

[*Exit* BRUTUS.

Well, Brutus, thou art noble; yet, I see,
Thy honourable mettle may be wrought

From that it is dispos'd: therefore 'tis meet
That noble minds keep ever with their likes;
For who so firm that cannot be seduced?
Cæsar doth bear me hard; but he loves Brutus:
If I were Brutus now, and he were Cassius,
He should not humour me. I will this night,
In several hands, in at his windows throw,
As if they came from several citizens,
Writings, all tending to the great opinion
That Rome holds of his name; wherein obscurely
Cæsar's ambition shall be glanced at:
And, after this, let Cæsar seat him sure;
For we will shake him, or worse days endure.

                                             [Exit.

SCENE III

The same. A street.

Thunder and lightning. Enter, from opposite sides, CASCA,
with his sword drawn, and CICERO.

CICERO

Good even, Casca: brought you Cæsar home?
Why are you breathless? and why stare you so?

CASCA

Are not you mov'd, when all the sway of earth
Shakes like a thing unfirm? O Cicero,
I have seen tempests, when the scolding winds
Have riv'd the knotty oaks; and I have seen
Th'ambitious ocean swell and rage and foam,
To be exalted with the threat'ning clouds:
But never till to-night, never till now,
Did I go through a tempest dropping fire.
Either there is a civil strife in heaven,
Or else the world, too saucy with the gods,
Incenses them to send destruction.

CICERO

Why, saw you any thing more wonderful?

CASCA

A common slave — you know him well by sight —
Held up his left hand, which did flame and burn
Like twenty torches join'd; and yet his hand,
Not sensible of fire, remain'd unscorch'd.
Besides, — I ha' not since put up my sword, —
Against the Capitol I met a lion,
Who glared upon me, and went surly by,
Without annoying me: and there were drawn
Upon a heap a hundred ghastly women,
Transformed with their fear; who swore they saw
Men, all in fire, walk up and down the streets.
And yesterday the bird of night did sit
Even at noonday upon the market-place,
Hooting and shrieking. When these prodigies
Do so conjointly meet, let not men say,
'These are their reasons, — they are natural';
For, I believe, they are portentous things
Unto the climate that they point upon.

CICERO

Indeed, it is a strange-disposed time:
But men may construe things after their fashion,
Clean from the purpose of the things themselves.
Comes Cæsar to the Capitol to-morrow?

CASCA

He doth: for he did bid Antonius
Send word to you he would be there to-morrow.

CICERO

Good night, then, Casca: this disturbed sky
Is not to walk in.

CASCA

        Farewell, Cicero.   [*Exit* CICERO.

          Enter CASSIUS.

CASSIUS

Who's there?

CASCA
       A Roman.

CASSIUS
             Casca, by your voice.

CASCA
Your ear is good. Cassius, what night is this!

CASSIUS
A very pleasing night to honest men.

CASCA
Who ever knew the heavens menace so?

CASSIUS
Those that have known the earth so full of faults.
For my part, I have walk'd about the streets,
Submitting me unto the perilous night;
And, thus unbraced, Casca, as you see,
Have bared my bosom to the thunder-stone:
And when the cross blue lightning seem'd to open
The breast of heaven, I did present myself
Even in the aim and very flash of it.

CASCA
But wherefore did you so much tempt the heavens?
It is the part of men to fear and tremble,
When the most mighty gods by tokens send
Such dreadful heralds to astonish us.

CASSIUS
You are dull, Casca; and those sparks of life
That should be in a Roman you do want,
Or else you use not. You look pale, and gaze,
And put on fear, and cast yourself in wonder,
To see the strange impatience of the heavens:
But if you would consider the true cause
Why all these fires, why all these gliding ghosts,
Why birds and beasts from quality and kind —
Why old men, fools, and children calculate;
Why all these things change from their ordinance,
Their natures, and pre-formed faculties,
To monstrous quality; — why, you shall find

That heaven hath infus'd them with these spirits,
To make them instruments of fear and warning
Unto some monstrous state.
Now could I, Casca, name to thee a man
Most like this dreadful night,
That thunders, lightens, opens graves, and roars
As doth the lion in the Capitol, —
A man no mightier than thyself or me
In personal action; yet prodigious grown,
And fearful, as these strange eruptions are.

CASCA

'Tis Cæsar that you mean; is it not, Cassius?

CASSIUS

Let it be who it is; for Romans now
Have thews and limbs like to their ancestors;
But, woe the while! our fathers' minds are dead,
And we are govern'd with our mothers' spirits;
Our yoke and sufferance show us womanish.

CASCA

Indeed, they say the senators to-morrow
Mean to establish Cæsar as a king;
And he shall wear his crown by sea and land,
In every place, save here in Italy.

CASSIUS

I know where I will wear this dagger, then;
Cassius from bondage will deliver Cassius:
Therein, ye gods, you make the weak most strong;
Therein, ye gods, you tyrants do defeat:
Nor stony tower, nor walls of beaten brass,
Nor airless dungeon, nor strong links of iron,
Can be retentive to the strength of spirit;
But life, being weary of these worldly bars,
Never lacks power to dismiss itself.
If I know this, know all the world besides,
That part of tyranny that I do bear
I can shake off at pleasure.

[*Thunder still.*

CASCA

So can I:
So every bondman in his own hand bears
The power to cancel his captivity.

CASSIUS

And why should Cæsar be a tyrant, then?
Poor man! I know he would not be a wolf,
But that he sees the Romans are but sheep:
He were no lion, were not Romans hinds.
Those that with haste will make a mighty fire
Begin it with weak straws: what trash is Rome,
What rubbish, and what offal, when it serves
For the base matter to illuminate
So vile a thing as Cæsar! But, O grief,
Where hast thou led me? I perhaps speak this
Before a willing bondman: then I know
My answer must be made; but I am arm'd,
And dangers are to me indifferent.

CASCA

You speak to Casca; and to such a man
That is no fleering tell-tale. Hold, my hand:
Be factious for redress of all these griefs;
And I will set this foot of mine as far
As who goes farthest.

CASSIUS

There's a bargain made.
Now know you, Casca, I have mov'd already
Some certain of the noblest-minded Romans
To undergo with me an enterprise
Of honourable-dangerous consequence;
And I do know, by this, they stay for me
In Pompey's porch: for now, this fearful night,
There is no stir or walking in the streets;
And the complexion of the element
In's favour's like the work we have in hand,
Most bloody, fiery and most terrible.

CASCA

Stand close awhile, for here comes one in haste.

CASSIUS

'Tis Cinna, — I do know him by his gait;
He is a friend.

Enter CINNA.

Cinna, where haste you so?

CINNA

To find out you. Who's that? Metellus Cimber?

CASSIUS

No, it is Casca; one incorporate
To our attempts. Am I not stay'd for, Cinna?

CINNA

I am glad on't. What a fearful night is this!
There's two or three of us have seen strange sights.

CASSIUS

Am I not stay'd for? tell me.

CINNA

                              Yes, you are. —

O Cassius, if you could
But win the noble Brutus to our party —

CASSIUS

Be you content: good Cinna, take this paper,
And look you lay it in the prætor's chair,
Where Brutus may but find it; and throw this
In at his window; set this up with wax
Upon old Brutus' statue: all this done,
Repair to Pompey's porch, where you shall find us.
Is Decius Brutus and Trebonius there?

CINNA

All but Metellus Cimber; and he's gone
To seek you at your house. Well, I will hie,
And so bestow these papers as you bade me.

CASSIUS

That done, repair to Pompey's theatre.   [*Exit* CINNA.
Come, Casca, you and I will yet, ere day,
See Brutus at his house: three parts of him
Is ours already; and the man entire,
Upon the next encounter, yields him ours.

CASCA

O, he sits high in all the people's hearts:
And that which would appear offence in us,
His countenance, like richest alchemy,
Will change to virtue and to worthiness.

CASSIUS

Him, and his worth, and our great need of him,
You have right well conceited. Let us go,
For it is after midnight; and, ere day,
We will awake him, and be sure of him.

[*Exeunt.*

ACT II

SCENE I

Rome. BRUTUS' *orchard.*

Enter BRUTUS.

BRUTUS
What, Lucius, ho! —
I cannot, by the progress of the stars,
Give guess how near to day. — Lucius, I say! —
I would it were my fault to sleep so soundly. —
When, Lucius, when? awake, I say! what, Lucius!

Enter LUCIUS.

LUCIUS
Call'd you, my lord?

BRUTUS
Get me a taper in my study, Lucius:
When it is lighted, come and call me here.

LUCIUS
I will, my lord.

[*Exit.*

BRUTUS
It must be by his death: and, for my part,
I know no personal cause to spurn at him,
But for the general. He would be crown'd: —
How that might change his nature, there's the question:
It is the bright day that brings forth the adder;
And that craves wary walking. Crown him? — that; —
And then, I grant, we put a sting in him,
That at his will he may do danger with.
Th'abuse of greatness is, when it disjoins
Remorse from power: and, to speak truth of Cæsar,
I have not known when his affections sway'd
More than his reason. But 'tis a common proof,
That lowliness is young ambition's ladder,

Whereto the climber-upward turns his face;
But when he once attains the upmost round,
He then unto the ladder turns his back,
Looks in the clouds, scorning the base degrees
By which he did ascend: so Cæsar may;
Then, lest he may, prevent. And, since the quarrel
Will bear no colour for the thing he is,
Fashion it thus: that what he is, augmented,
Would run to these and these extremities:
And therefore think him as a serpent's egg,
Which, hatch'd, would, as his kind, grow mischievous;
And kill him in the shell.

Re-enter LUCIUS.

LUCIUS

The taper burneth in your closet, sir.
Searching the window for a flint, I found
                              [*Gives him the letter.*
This paper, thus seal'd up; and, I am sure,
It did not lie there when I went to bed.

BRUTUS

Get you to bed again; it is not day.
Is not to-morrow, boy, the ides of March?

LUCIUS

I know not, sir.

BRUTUS

Look in the calendar, and bring me word.

LUCIUS

I will, sir.

                                        [*Exit.*

BRUTUS

The exhalations, whizzing in the air,
Give so much light, that I may read by them.
                      [*Opens the letter and reads.*
'Brutus, thou sleep'st; awake, and see thyself.
Shall Rome, etc. Speak, strike, redress!' —
'Brutus, thou sleep'st: awake!' —

25

Such instigations have been often dropp'd
Where I have took them up.
'Shall Rome, etc.' Thus must I piece it out;
Shall Rome stand under one man's awe? What, Rome?
My ancestors did from the streets of Rome
The Tarquin drive, when he was call'd a king.
'Speak, strike, redress!' — Am I entreated
To speak and strike? O Rome, I make thee promise,
If the redress will follow, thou receivest
Thy full petition at the hand of Brutus!

Enter LUCIUS.

LUCIUS

Sir, March is wasted fifteen days.

[*Knock without.*

BRUTUS

'Tis good. Go to the gate; somebody knocks,

[*Exit* LUCIUS.

Since Cassius first did whet me against Cæsar,
I have not slept.
Between the acting of a dreadful thing
And the first motion, all the interim is
Like a phantasma or a hideous dream:
The Genius and the mortal instruments
Are then in council; and the state of man,
Like to a little kingdom, suffers then
The nature of an insurrection.

Re-enter LUCIUS.

LUCIUS

Sir, 'tis your brother Cassius at the door,
Who doth desire to see you.

BRUTUS

               Is he alone?

LUCIUS

No, sir, there are more with him.

BRUTUS

                 Do you know them?

LUCIUS

No, sir; their hats are pluck'd about their ears,
And half their faces buried in their cloaks,
That by no means I may discover them
By any mark of favour.

BRUTUS

               Let 'em enter.

                             [Exit LUCIUS.

They are the faction. O conspiracy,
Shamest thou to show thy dangerous brow by night,
When evils are most free? O, then, by day
Where wilt thou find a cavern dark enough
To mask thy monstrous visage? Seek none, conspiracy;
Hide it in smiles and affability:
For if thou put thy native semblance on,
Not Erebus itself were dim enough
To hide thee from prevention.

   Enter the Conspirators, CASSIUS, CASCA, DECIUS,
   CINNA, METELLUS CIMBER, *and* TREBONIUS.

CASSIUS

I think we are too bold upon your rest:
Good morrow, Brutus; do we trouble you?

BRUTUS

I have been up this hour; awake all night.
Know I these men that come along with you?

CASSIUS

Yes, every man of them; and no man here
But honours you; and every one doth wish
You had but that opinion of yourself
Which every noble Roman bears of you. —
This is Trebonius.

BRUTUS

              He is welcome hither.

CASSIUS

This, Decius Brutus.

BRUTUS

              He is welcome too.

CASSIUS
This, Casca; this, Cinna; and this, Metellus Cimber.

BRUTUS
They are all welcome. —
What watchful cares do interpose themselves
Betwixt your eyes and night?

CASSIUS
Shall I entreat a word?

[Brutus and Cassius retire.

DECIUS
Here lies the east: doth not the day break here?

CASCA
No.

CINNA
O, pardon, sir, it doth; and yon grey lines
That fret the clouds are messengers of day.

CASCA
You shall confess that you are both deceived.
Here, as I point my sword, the sun arises;
Which is a great way growing on the south,
Weighing the youthful season of the year.
Some two months hence, up higher toward the north
He first presents his fire; and the high east
Stands, as the Capitol, directly here.

BRUTUS
[*Advancing*] Give me your hands all over, one by one.

CASSIUS
[*Advancing*] And let us swear our resolution.

BRUTUS
No, not an oath: if not the face of men,
The sufferance of our souls, the time's abuse, —
If these be motives weak, break off betimes,
And every man hence to his idle bed;
So let high-sighted tyranny range on,
Till each man drop by lottery. But if these,
As I am sure they do, bear fire enough
To kindle cowards, and to steel with valour

The melting spirits of women; then, countrymen,
What need we any spur, but our own cause,
To prick us to redress? what other bond
Than secret Romans, that have spoke the word,
And will not palter? and what other oath
Than honesty to honesty engaged,
That this shall be, or we will fall for it?
Swear priests, and cowards, and men cautelous,
Old feeble carrions, and such suffering souls
That welcome wrongs; unto bad causes swear
Such creatures as men doubt: but do not stain
The even virtue of our enterprise,
Nor th'insuppressive mettle of our spirits,
To think that or our cause or our performance
Did need an oath; when every drop of blood
That every Roman bears, and nobly bears,
Is guilty of a several bastardy,
If he do break the smallest particle
Of any promise that hath pass'd from him.

CASSIUS

But what of Cicero? shall we sound him?
I think he will stand very strong with us.

CASCA

Let us not leave him out.

CINNA

                No, by no means.

METELLUS

O, let us have him; for his silver hairs
Will purchase us a good opinion,
And buy men's voices to commend our deeds:
It shall be said, his judgement rul'd our hands;
Our youths and wildness shall no whit appear,
But all be buried in his gravity.

BRUTUS

O, name him not: let us not break with him;
For he will never follow any thing
That other men begin.

CASSIUS

             Then leave him out.

CASCA
  Indeed he is not fit.

DECIUS

Shall no man else be touch'd but only Cæsar?

CASSIUS

Decius, well urg'd: — I think it is not meet,
Mark Antony, so well belov'd of Cæsar,
Should outlive Cæsar: we shall find of him
A shrewd contriver; and, you know, his means,
If he improve them, may well stretch so far
As to annoy us all: which to prevent,
Let Antony and Cæsar fall together.

BRUTUS

Our course will seem too bloody, Caius Cassius,
To cut the head off, and then hack the limbs, —
Like wrath in death, and envy afterwards;
For Antony is but a limb of Cæsar:
Let's be sacrificers, but not butchers, Caius.
We all stand up against the spirit of Cæsar;
And in the spirit of men there is no blood:
O, that we, then, could come by Cæsar's spirit,
And not dismember Cæsar! But, alas,
Cæsar must bleed for it! And, gentle friends,
Let's kill him boldly, but not wrathfully;
Let's carve him as a dish fit for the gods,
Not hew him as a carcass fit for hounds:
And let our hearts, as subtle masters do,
Stir up their servants to an act of rage,
And after seem to chide 'em. This shall make
Our purpose necessary, and not envious:
Which so appearing to the common eyes,
We shall be call'd purgers, not murderers.
And for Mark Antony, think not of him;
For he can do no more than Cæsar's arm
When Cæsar's head is off.

CASSIUS

                    Yet I fear him;
For in the ingrafted love he bears to Cæsar —

BRUTUS

Alas, good Cassius, do not think of him:
If he love Cæsar, all that he can do
Is to himself, — take thought, and die for Cæsar:
And that were much he should; for he is given
To sports, to wildness, and much company.

TREBONIUS

There is no fear in him; let him not die;
For he will live, and laugh at this hereafter.

[*Clock strikes.*

BRUTUS

Peace! count the clock.

CASSIUS

The clock hath stricken three.

TREBONIUS

'Tis time to part.

CASSIUS

But it is doubtful yet,
Whether Cæsar will come forth to-day or no;
For he is superstitious grown of late;
Quite from the main opinion he held once
Of fantasy, of dreams, and ceremonies:
It may be, these apparent prodigies,
The unaccustom'd terror of this night,
And the persuasion of his augurers,
May hold him from the Capitol to-day.

DECIUS

Never fear that: if he be so resolved,
I can o'ersway him; for he loves to hear
That unicorns may be betray'd with trees,
And bears with glasses, elephants with holes,
Lions with toils, and men with flatterers:
But when I tell him he hates flatterers,
He says he does, — being then most flattered.
Let me work;
For I can give his humour the true bent,
And I will bring him to the Capitol.

CASSIUS
  Nay, we will all of us be there to fetch him.

BRUTUS
  By the eighth hour: is that the uttermost?

CINNA
  Be that the uttermost, and fail not then.

METELLUS
  Caius Ligarius doth bear Cæsar hard,
  Who rated him for speaking well of Pompey:
  I wonder none of you have thought of him.

BRUTUS
  Now, good Metellus, go along by him:
  He loves me well, and I have given him reasons;
  Send him but hither, and I'll fashion him.

CASSIUS
  The morning comes upon's: we'll leave you, Brutus: —
  And, friends, disperse yourselves; but all remember
  What you have said, and show yourselves true Romans.

BRUTUS
  Good gentlemen, look fresh and merrily;
  Let not our looks put on our purposes;
  But bear it as our Roman actors do,
  With untired spirits and formal constancy:
  And so, good morrow to you every one.
                    [*Exeunt all but* BRUTUS.
  Boy! Lucius! — Fast asleep? It is no matter;
  Enjoy the honey-heavy dew of slumber:
  Thou hast no figures nor no fantasies,
  Which busy care draws in the brains of men;
  Therefore thou sleep'st so sound.

                    Enter PORTIA.

PORTIA
                    Brutus, my lord!

BRUTUS
  Portia, what mean you? wherefore rise you now?
  It is not for your health thus to commit
  Your weak condition to the raw-cold morning.

33

PORTIA

Nor for yours neither. Y' have ungently, Brutus,
Stole from my bed: and yesternight, at supper,
You suddenly arose, and walk'd about,
Musing and sighing, with your arms across;
And when I ask'd you what the matter was,
You stared upon me with ungentle looks:
I urg'd you further; then you scratch'd your head,
And too impatiently stamp'd with your foot:
Yet I insisted, yet you answer'd not;
But, with an angry wafture of your hand,
Gave sign for me to leave you: so I did;
Fearing to strengthen that impatience
Which seem'd too much enkindled; and withal
Hoping it was but an effect of humour,
Which sometime hath his hour with every man.
It will not let you eat, nor talk, nor sleep;
And, could it work so much upon your shape,
As it hath much prevail'd on your condition,
I should not know you, Brutus. Dear my lord,
Make me acquainted with your cause of grief.

BRUTUS

I am not well in health, and that is all.

PORTIA

Brutus is wise, and, were he not in health,
He would embrace the means to come by it.

BRUTUS

Why, so I do. — Good Portia, go to bed.

PORTIA

Is Brutus sick, — and is it physical
To walk unbraced, and suck up the humours
Of the dank morning? What, is Brutus sick, —
And will he steal out of his wholesome bed,
To dare the vile contagion of the night,
And tempt the rheumy and unpurged air
To add unto his sickness? No, my Brutus;
You have some sick offence within your mind,

Which, by the right and virtue of my place,
I ought to know of: and, upon my knees,
I charm you, by my once-commended beauty,
By all your vows of love, and that great vow
Which did incorporate and make us one,
That you unfold to me, yourself, your half,
Why you are heavy; and what men to-night
Have had resort to you, — for here have been
Some six or seven, who did hide their faces
Even from darkness.

BRUTUS

          Kneel not, gentle Portia.

PORTIA

I should not need, if you were gentle Brutus.
Within the bond of marriage, tell me, Brutus,
Is it excepted I should know no secrets
That appertain to you? Am I yourself
But, as it were, in sort or limitation, —
To keep with you at meals, comfort your bed,
And talk to you sometimes? Dwell I but in the suburbs
Of your good pleasure? If it be no more,
Portia is Brutus' harlot, not his wife.

BRUTUS

You are my true and honourable wife;
As dear to me as are the ruddy drops
That visit my sad heart.

PORTIA

If this were true, then should I know this secret.
I grant I am a woman; but withal
A woman that Lord Brutus took to wife:
I grant I am a woman; but withal
A woman well-reputed, — Cato's daughter.
Think you I am no stronger than my sex,
Being so father'd and so husbanded?
Tell me your counsels; I will not disclose 'em:
I have made strong proof of my constancy,
Giving myself a voluntary wound

PORTIA Tell me your counsels; I will not disclose 'em.

Here, in the thigh: can I bear that with patience,
And not my husband's secrets?

BRUTUS

O ye gods,
Render me worthy of this noble wife!

[*Knocking without.*

Hark, hark! one knocks: Portia, go in awhile;
And by and by thy bosom shall partake
The secrets of my heart:
All my engagements I will construe to thee,
All the charactery of my sad brows: —
Leave me with haste. [*Exit* PORTIA.] — Lucius, who's
that knocks?

Enter LUCIUS *with* LIGARIUS.

LUCIUS

Here is a sick man that would speak with you.

BRUTUS

Caius Ligarius, that Metellus spake of. —
Boy, stand aside. — Caius Ligarius, — how!

LIGARIUS

Vouchsafe good-morrow from a feeble tongue.

BRUTUS

O, what a time have you chose out, brave Caius,
To wear a kerchief! Would you were not sick!

LIGARIUS

I am not sick, if Brutus have in hand
Any exploit worthy the name of honour.

BRUTUS

Such an exploit have I in hand, Ligarius,
Had you a healthful ear to hear of it.

LIGARIUS

By all the gods that Romans bow before,
I here discard my sickness! Soul of Rome!
Brave son, deriv'd from honourable loins!
Thou, like an exorcist, hast conjur'd up
My mortified spirit. Now bid me run,

37

And I will strive with things impossible;
Yea, get the better of them. What's to do?

BRUTUS

A piece of work that will make sick men whole.

LIGARIUS

But are not some whole that we must make sick?

BRUTUS

That must we also. What it is, my Caius,
I shall unfold to thee, as we are going
To whom it must be done.

LIGARIUS

         Set on your foot;
And, with a heart new-fired, I follow you,
To do I know not what: but it sufficeth
That Brutus leads me on.

BRUTUS

         Follow me, then.   *[Exeunt.*

SCENE II

The same. A hall in CAESAR'S *palace.*

Thunder and lightning. Enter JULIUS CAESAR, *in his nightgown.*

CAESAR

Nor heaven nor earth have been at peace to-night:
Thrice hath Calphurnia in her sleep cried out,
'Help, ho! they murder Cæsar!' — Who's within?

         Enter a SERVANT.

SERVANT

My lord?

CAESAR

Go bid the priests do present sacrifice,
And bring me their opinions of success.

SERVANT

I will, my lord.

         [Exit.

Enter CALPHURNIA.

CALPHURNIA

What mean you, Cæsar? think you to walk forth?
You shall not stir out of your house to-day.

CAESAR

Cæsar shall forth: the things that threaten'd me
Ne'er look'd but on my back; when they shall see
The face of Cæsar, they are vanished.

CALPHURNIA

Cæsar, I never stood on ceremonies,
Yet now they fright me. There is one within,
Besides the things that we have heard and seen,
Recounts most horrid sights seen by the watch.
A lioness hath whelped in the streets;
And graves have yawn'd, and yielded up their dead;
Fierce fiery warriors fight upon the clouds,
In ranks and squadrons and right form of war,
Which drizzled blood upon the Capitol;
The noise of battle hurtled in the air;
Horses did neigh, and dying men did groan;
And ghosts did shriek and squeal about the streets.
O Cæsar, these things are beyond all use,
And I do fear them!

CAESAR

                        What can be avoided
Whose end is purpos'd by the mighty gods?
Yet Cæsar shall go forth; for these predictions
Are to the world in general as to Cæsar.

CALPHURNIA

When beggars die, there are no comets seen;
The heavens themselves blaze forth the death of princes.

CAESAR

Cowards die many times before their deaths;
The valiant never taste of death but once.
Of all the wonders that I yet have heard,
It seems to me most strange that men should fear;
Seeing that death, a necessary end,
Will come when it will come.

Re-enter SERVANT.
>What say the augurers?

SERVANT

They would not have you to stir forth to-day.
Plucking the entrails of an offering forth,
They could not find a heart within the beast.

CAESAR

The gods do this in shame of cowardice:
Cæsar should be a beast without a heart,
If he should stay at home to-day for fear.
No, Cæsar shall not: danger knows full well
That Cæsar is more dangerous than he:
We are two lions litter'd in one day,
And I the elder and more terrible: —
And Cæsar shall go forth.

CALPHURNIA
>Alas, my lord,

Your wisdom is consum'd in confidence.
Do not go forth to-day: call it my fear
That keeps you in the house, and not your own.
We'll send Mark Antony to the senate-house;
And he shall say you are not well to-day:
Let me, upon my knee, prevail in this.

CAESAR

Mark Antony shall say I am not well;
And, for thy humour, I will stay at home.
>*Enter* DECIUS.

Here's Decius Brutus, he shall tell them so.

DECIUS

Cæsar, all hail! good morrow, worthy Cæsar:
I come to fetch you to the senate-house.

CAESAR

And you are come in very happy time,
To bear my greeting to the senators,
And tell them that I will not come to-day;
Cannot, is false; and that I dare not, falser:
I will not come to-day, — tell them so, Decius.

CALPHURNIA

Say he is sick.

CAESAR

       Shall Cæsar send a lie?
Have I in conquest stretch'd mine arm so far
To be afeard to tell greybeards the truth?
Decius, go tell them Cæsar will not come.

DECIUS

Most mighty Cæsar, let me know some cause,
Lest I be laugh'd at when I tell them so.

CAESAR

The cause is in my will, — I will not come;
That is enough to satisfy the senate.
But, for your private satisfaction,
Because I love you, I will let you know, —
Calphurnia here, my wife, stays me at home:
She dream'd to-night she saw my statua,
Which, like a fountain with an hundred spouts,
Did run pure blood; and many lusty Romans
Came smiling, and did bathe their hands in it:
And these does she apply for warnings and portents
And evils imminent; and on her knee
Hath begg'd that I will stay at home to-day.

DECIUS

This dream is all amiss interpreted;
It was a vision fair and fortunate:
Your statue spouting blood in many pipes,
In which so many smiling Romans bath'd,
Signifies that from you great Rome shall suck
Reviving blood; and that great men shall press
For tinctures, stains, relics, and recognisance.
This by Calphurnia's dream is signified.

CAESAR

And this way have you well expounded it.

DECIUS

I have, when you have heard what I can say:
And know it now, — the senate have concluded
To give, this day, a crown to mighty Cæsar.

If you shall send them word you will not come,
Their minds may change. Besides, it were a mock
Apt to be render'd, for some one to say,
'Break up the senate till another time,
When Cæsar's wife shall meet with better dreams.'
If Cæsar hide himself, shall they not whisper,
'Lo, Cæsar is afraid'?
Pardon me, Cæsar; for my dear dear love
To your proceeding bids me tell you this;
And reason to my love is liable.

CAESAR

How foolish do your fears seem now, Calphurnia!
I am ashamed I did yield to them. —
Give me my robe, for I will go: —

Enter PUBLIUS, BRUTUS, LIGARIUS, METELLUS,
CASCA, TREBONIUS, *and* CINNA.

And look where Publius is come to fetch me.

PUBLIUS

Good morrow, Cæsar.

CAESAR

Welcome, Publius. —
What, Brutus, are you stirr'd so early too? —
Good morrow, Casca. — Caius Ligarius,
Cæsar was ne'er so much your enemy
As that same ague which hath made you lean. —
What is't o'clock?

DECIUS

Cæsar, 'tis strucken eight.

CAESAR

I thank you for your pains and courtesy.

Enter ANTONY.

See! Antony, that revels long o' nights,
Is notwithstanding up. — Good morrow, Antony.

ANTONY

So to most noble Cæsar.

CAESAR

Bid them prepare within: —

I am to blame to be thus waited for. —
Now, Cinna: — now, Metellus: — what, Trebonius!
I have an hour's talk in store for you;
Remember that you call on me to-day:
Be near me, that I may remember you.

TREBONIUS

Cæsar, I will: — [*aside*] and so near will I be,
That your best friends shall wish I had been further.

CAESAR

Good friends, go in, and taste some wine with me;
And we, like friends, will straightway go together.

DECIUS [*aside*].

That every like is not the same, O Cæsar,
The heart of Brutus yearns to think upon!
    [*Exeunt.*

SCENE III

The same. A street near the Capitol.

Enter ARTEMIDORUS, *reading a paper.*

ARTEMIDORUS

Cæsar, beware of Brutus; take heed of Cassius; come
not near Casca; have an eye to Cinna; trust not
Trebonius; mark well Metellus Cimber; Decius Brutus
loves thee not: thou hast wrong'd Caius Ligarius. There
is but one mind in all these men, and it is bent against
Cæsar. If thou beest not immortal, look about you:
security gives way to conspiracy.
The mighty gods defend thee! Thy lover,
Here will I stand till Cæsar pass along,
And as a suitor will I give him this.
My heart laments that virtue cannot live
Out of the teeth of emulation.
If thou read this, O Cæsar, thou mayst live;
If not, the Fates with traitors do contrive.
                                            [*Exit.*

SCENE IV

The same. Another part of the same street, before the house of
BRUTUS.

Enter PORTIA *and* LUCIUS.

PORTIA

I prithee, boy, run to the senate-house;
Stay not to answer me, but get thee gone:
Why dost thou stay?

LUCIUS

           To know my errand, madam.

PORTIA

I would have had thee there, and here again,
Ere I can tell thee what thou shouldst do there. —
[*aside*] O constancy, be strong upon my side;
Set a huge mountain 'tween my heart and tongue!
I have a man's mind, but a woman's might.
How hard it is for women to keep counsel! —
Art thou here yet?

PORTIA How hard it is for women to keep counsel!.

44

LUCIUS
               Madam, what should I do?
Run to the Capitol, and nothing else?
And so return to you, and nothing else?

PORTIA
  Yes, bring me word, boy, if thy lord look well,
  For he went sickly forth: and take good note
  What Cæsar doth, what suitors press to him.
  Hark, boy! what noise is that?

LUCIUS
  I hear none, madam.

PORTIA
             Prithee, listen well:
  I heard a bustling rumour, like a fray,
  And the wind brings it from the Capitol.

LUCIUS
  Sooth, madam, I hear nothing.

Enter the SOOTHSAYER.

PORTIA
  Come hither, fellow: which way hast thou been?

SOOTHSAYER
  At mine own house, good lady.

PORTIA
  What is't o'clock?

SOOTHSAYER
            About the ninth hour, lady.

PORTIA
  Is Cæsar yet gone to the Capitol?

SOOTHSAYER
  Madam, not yet: I go to take my stand,
  To see him pass on to the Capitol.

PORTIA
  Thou hast some suit to Cæsar, hast thou not?

SOOTHSAYER
  That I have, lady: if it will please Cæsar
  To be so good to Cæsar as to hear me,
  I shall beseech him to befriend himself.

PORTIA

Why, know'st thou any harm's intended towards him?

SOOTHSAYER

None that I know will be, much that I fear may chance.
Good morrow to you. — Here the street is narrow:
The throng that follows Cæsar at the heels,
Of senators, of prætors, common suitors,
Will crowd a feeble man almost to death:
I'll get me to a place more void, and there
Speak to great Cæsar as he comes along.

[*Exit.*

PORTIA

I must go in. — [*aside*] Ay me, how weak a thing
The heart of woman is! O Brutus,
The heavens speed thee in thine enterprise! —
Sure, the boy heard me. — Brutus hath a suit
That Cæsar will not grant. — O, I grow faint. —
Run, Lucius, and commend me to my lord;
Say I am merry: come to me again,
And bring me word what he doth say to thee.

[*Exeunt severally.*

ACT III

SCENE I

Rome. Before the Capitol; the SENATE *sitting.*

A crowd of people; among them ARTEMIDORUS *and the*
SOOTHSAYER. *Flourish. Enter* CAESAR, BRUTUS,
CASSIUS, CASCA, DECIUS, METELLUS,
TREBONIUS, CINNA, ANTONY, LEPIDUS,
POPILIUS, PUBLIUS, *and others.*

CAESAR
The ides of March are come.

SOOTHSAYER
Ay, Cæsar; but not gone.

ARTEMIDORUS
Hail, Cæsar! read this schedule.

DECIUS
Trebonius doth desire you to o'er-read,
At your best leisure, this his humble suit.

ARTEMIDORUS
O Cæsar, read mine first; for mine's a suit
That touches Cæsar nearer; read it, great Cæsar.

CAESAR
What touches us ourself, shall be last serv'd.

ARTEMIDORUS
Delay not, Cæsar; read it instantly.

CAESAR
What, is the fellow mad?

PUBLIUS
             Sirrah, give place.

CASSIUS
What, urge you your petitions in the street?
Come to the Capitol.

    CAESAR *enters the Capitol, the rest following.*

All the SENATORS *rise.*

POPILIUS
I wish your enterprise to-day may thrive.

CASSIUS
What enterprise, Popilius?

POPILIUS
            Fare you well.   *[Advances to* CAESAR.

BRUTUS
What said Popilius Lena?

CASSIUS
He wish'd to-day our enterprise might thrive.
I fear our purpose is discovered.

BRUTUS
Look, how he makes to Cæsar: mark him.

CASSIUS
  Casca,
Be sudden, for we fear prevention. —
Brutus, what shall be done? If this be known,
Cassius or Cæsar never shall turn back,
For I will slay myself.

BRUTUS
          Cassius, be constant:
Popilius Lena speaks not of our purpose;
For, look, he smiles, and Cæsar doth not change.

CASSIUS
Trebonius knows his time; for, look you, Brutus,
He draws Mark Antony out of the way.

        [Exeunt ANTONY *and* TREBONIUS.
CAESAR *and the* SENATORS *take their seats.*

DECIUS
Where is Metellus Cimber? Let him go,
And presently prefer his suit to Cæsar.

BRUTUS
He is address'd: press near and second him.

CINNA

Casca, you are the first that rears your hand.

CAESAR

Are we all ready? What is now amiss
That Cæsar and his senate must redress?

METELLUS

Most high, most mighty, and most puissant Cæsar,
Metellus Cimber throws before thy seat
An humble heart, —

[*Kneeling.*

CAESAR

        I must prevent thee, Cimber.
These couchings and these lowly courtesies
Might fire the blood of ordinary men,
And turn pre-ordinance and first decree
Into the law of children. Be not fond,
To think that Cæsar bears such rebel blood
That will be thaw'd from the true quality
With that which melteth fools; I mean, sweet words,
Low-crooked curt'sies, and base spaniel-fawning.
Thy brother by decree is banished:
If thou dost bend, and pray, and fawn for him,
I spurn thee like a cur out of my way.
Know, Cæsar doth not wrong; nor without cause
Will he be satisfied.

METELLUS

Is there no voice more worthy than my own,
To sound more sweetly in great Cæsar's ear
For the repealing of my banish'd brother?

BRUTUS

I kiss thy hand, but not in flattery, Cæsar;
Desiring thee that Publius Cimber may
Have an immediate freedom of repeal.

CAESAR

What, Brutus!

CASSIUS

    Pardon, Cæsar; Cæsar, pardon:
As low as to thy foot doth Cassius fall,
To beg enfranchisement for Publius Cimber.

CAESAR

I could be well mov'd, if I were as you;
If I could pray to move, prayers would move me:
But I am constant as the northern star,
Of whose true-fix'd and resting quality
There is no fellow in the firmament.
The skies are painted with unnumber'd sparks;
They are all fire, and every one doth shine;
But there's but one in all doth hold his place:
So in the world, — 'tis furnish'd well with men,
And men are flesh and blood, and apprehensive;
Yet in the number I do know but one
That unassailable holds on his rank,
Unshak'd of motion: and that I am he,
Let me a little show it, even in this, —
That I was constant Cimber should be banish'd,
And constant do remain to keep him so.

CINNA

O Cæsar, —

CAESAR

    Hence! wilt thou lift up Olympus?

DECIUS

Great Cæsar, —

CAESAR

    Doth not Brutus bootless kneel?

CASCA

Speak, hands, for me!

        [*They stab* CAESAR.

CAESAR

Et tu, Brute? — Then fall, Cæsar!
   [*Dies. The senators and people retire in confusion.*

CINNA

Liberty! Freedom! Tyranny is dead! —
Run hence, proclaim, cry it about the streets.

CASSIUS

Some to the common pulpits, and cry out,
'Liberty, freedom, and enfranchisement!'

BRUTUS

People, and senators, be not affrighted;
Fly not; stand still: — ambition's debt is paid.

CASCA

Go to the pulpit, Brutus.

DECIUS

     And Cassius too.

BRUTUS

Where's Publius?

CINNA

Here, quite confounded with this mutiny.

METELLUS

Stand fast together, lest some friend of Cæsar's
Should chance —

BRUTUS

Talk not of standing. — Publius, good cheer;
There is no harm intended to your person,
Nor to no Roman else: so tell them, Publius.

CASSIUS

And leave us, Publius; lest that the people,
Rushing on us, should do your age some mischief.

BRUTUS

Do so: — and let no man abide this deed,
But we the doers.

Re-enter TREBONIUS.

CASSIUS

Where is Antony?

TREBONIUS

    Fled to his house amazed:
Men, wives, and children stare, cry out, and run
As it were doomsday.

BRUTUS
                    Fates, we will know your pleasures: —
That we shall die, we know; 'tis but the time,
And drawing days out, that men stand upon.

CASSIUS
Why, he that cuts off twenty years of life
Cuts off so many years of fearing death.

BRUTUS
Grant that, and then is death a benefit:
So are we Cæsar's friends, that have abridg'd
His time of fearing death. — Stoop, Romans, stoop,
And let us bathe our hands in Cæsar's blood
Up to the elbows, and besmear our swords:
Then walk we forth, even to the market-place,
And, waving our red weapons o'er our heads,
Let's all cry 'Peace, freedom, and liberty!'

CASSIUS
Stoop, then, and wash. — How many ages hence
Shall this our lofty scene be acted over
In states unborn and accents yet unknown!

BRUTUS
How many times shall Cæsar bleed in sport,
That now on Pompey's basis lies along
No worthier than the dust!

CASSIUS
                    So oft as that shall be,
So often shall the knot of us be call'd
The men that gave their country liberty.

DECIUS
What, shall we forth?

CASSIUS
                    Ay, every man away:
Brutus shall lead; and we will grace his heels
With the most boldest and best hearts of Rome.

BRUTUS
Soft! who comes here?
                    Enter a SERVANT.
                    A friend of Antony's.

52

SERVANT

Thus, Brutus, did my master bid me kneel;
Thus did Mark Antony bid me fall down;
And, being prostrate, thus he bade me say: —
Brutus is noble, wise, valiant, and honest;
Cæsar was mighty, bold, royal, and loving:
Say I love Brutus, and I honour him;
Say I fear'd Cæsar, honour'd him, and lov'd him.
If Brutus will vouchsafe that Antony
May safely come to him, and be resolv'd
How Cæsar hath deserv'd to lie in death,
Mark Antony shall not love Cæsar dead
So well as Brutus living; but will follow
The fortunes and affairs of noble Brutus
Through the hazards of this untrod state
With all true faith. So says my master Antony.

BRUTUS

Thy master is a wise and valiant Roman;
I never thought him worse.
Tell him, so please him come unto this place,
He shall be satisfied; and, by my honour,
Depart untouch'd.

SERVANT

     I'll fetch him presently.   [*Exit.*

BRUTUS

I know that we shall have him well to friend.

CASSIUS

I wish we may: but yet have I a mind
That fears him much; and my misgiving still
Falls shrewdly to the purpose.

BRUTUS

But here comes Antony.
     Re-enter ANTONY.
      Welcome, Mark Antony.

ANTONY

O mighty Cæsar! dost thou lie so low?
Are all thy conquests, glories, triumphs, spoils,
Shrunk to this little measure? Fare thee well. —

I know not, gentlemen, what you intend,
Who else must be let blood, who else is rank:
If I myself, there is no hour so fit
As Cæsar's death's hour: nor no instrument
Of half that worth as those your swords, made rich
With the most noble blood of all this world.
I do beseech ye, if you bear me hard,
Now, whilst your purpled hands do reek and smoke,
Fulfil your pleasure. Live a thousand years,
I shall not find myself so apt to die:
No place will please me so, no mean of death
As here by Cæsar, and by you cut off,
The choice and master spirits of this age.

BRUTUS

O Antony, beg not your death of us.
Though now we must appear bloody and cruel,
As, by our hands and this our present act,
You see we do; yet see you but our hands,
And this the bleeding business they have done:
Our hearts you see not, — they are pitiful;
And pity to the general wrong of Rome —
As fire drives out fire, so pity pity —
Hath done this deed on Cæsar. For your part,
To you our swords have leaden points, Mark Antony,
Our arms no strength of malice; and our hearts,
Of brothers' temper, do receive you in
With all kind love, good thoughts, and reverence.

CASSIUS

Your voice shall be as strong as any man's
In the disposing of new dignities.

BRUTUS

Only be patient till we have appeased
The multitude, beside themselves with fear,
And then we will deliver you the cause,
Why I, that did love Cæsar when I struck him,
Have thus proceeded.

ANTONY
                    I doubt not of your wisdom.
Let each man render me his bloody hand:
First, Marcus Brutus, will I shake with you: —
Next, Caius Cassius, do I take your hand; —
Now, Decius Brutus, yours; — now yours, Metellus; —
Yours, Cinna; — and, my valiant Casca, yours; —
Though last, not least in love, yours, good Trebonius.
Gentlemen all, — alas, what shall I say?
My credit now stands on such slippery ground,
That one of two bad ways you must conceit me,
Either a coward or a flatterer. —
That I did love thee, Cæsar, O, 'tis true:
If, then, thy spirit look upon us now,
Shall it not grieve thee dearer than thy death,
To see thy Antony making his peace,
Shaking the bloody fingers of thy foes,
Most noble! in the presence of thy corse?
Had I as many eyes as thou hast wounds,
Weeping as fast as they stream forth thy blood,
It would become me better than to close
In terms of friendship with thine enemies.
Pardon me, Julius! — Here wast thou bay'd, brave hart;
Here didst thou fall; and here thy hunters stand,
Sign'd in thy spoil, and crimson'd in thy lethe. —
O world, thou wast the forest to this hart;
And this, indeed, O world, the heart of thee. —
How like a deer, strucken by many princes,
Dost thou here lie!

CASSIUS
Mark Antony, —

ANTONY
                    Pardon me, Caius Cassius:
The enemies of Cæsar shall say this;
Then, in a friend, it is cold modesty.

CASSIUS
I blame you not for praising Cæsar so;
But what compact mean you to have with us?

ANTONY How like a deer, strucken by many princes, dost thou here lie!

Will you be prick'd in number of our friends;
Or shall we on, and not depend on you?

ANTONY
Therefore I took your hands; but was, indeed,
Sway'd from the point, by looking down on Cæsar.
Friends am I with you all, and love you all;
Upon this hope, that you shall give me reasons
Why and wherein Cæsar was dangerous.

BRUTUS
Or else were this a savage spectacle:
Our reasons are so full of good regard,
That were you, Antony, the son of Cæsar,
You should be satisfied.

ANTONY

That's all I seek:
And am moreover suitor that I may
Produce his body to the market-place;
And in the pulpit, as becomes a friend,
Speak in the order of his funeral.

BRUTUS

You shall, Mark Antony.

CASSIUS

Brutus, a word with you.
[aside to BRUTUS] You know not what you do: do not
   consent
That Antony speak in his funeral:
Know you how much the people may be mov'd
By that which he will utter?

BRUTUS [aside to CASSIUS].

By your pardon; —
I will myself into the pulpit first,
And show the reason of our Cæsar's death:
What Antony shall speak, I will protest
He speaks by leave and by permission;
And that we are contented Cæsar shall
Have all true rites and lawful ceremonies.
It shall advantage more than do us wrong.

CASSIUS

I know not what may fall; I like it not.

BRUTUS

Mark Antony, here, take you Cæsar's body.
You shall not in your funeral speech blame us,
But speak all good you can devise of Cæsar;
And say you do't by our permission;
Else shall you not have any hand at all
About his funeral: and you shall speak
In the same pulpit whereto I am going,
After my speech is ended.

ANTONY

Be it so;
I do desire no more.

BRUTUS

Prepare the body, then, and follow us.

[*Exeunt all but* ANTONY.

ANTONY

O, pardon me, thou bleeding piece of earth,
That I am meek and gentle with these butchers!
Thou art the ruins of the noblest man
That ever lived in the tide of times.
Woe to the hand that shed this costly blood!
Over thy wounds now do I prophesy, —
Which, like dumb mouths, do ope their ruby lips,
To beg the voice and utterance of my tongue, —
A curse shall light upon the limbs of men;
Domestic fury and fierce civil strife
Shall cumber all the parts of Italy;
Blood and destruction shall be so in use,
And dreadful objects so familiar,
That mothers shall but smile when they behold
Their infants quarter'd with the hands of war;
All pity chok'd with custom of fell deeds:
And Cæsar's spirit, ranging for revenge,
With Ate by his side come hot from hell,
Shall in these confines with a monarch's voice
Cry 'Havoc,' and let slip the dogs of war;
That this foul deed shall smell above the earth
With carriovn men, groaning for burial.

Enter OCTAVIUS' SERVANT.

You serve Octavius Cæsar, do you not?

SERVANT

I do, Mark Antony.

ANTONY

Cæsar did write for him to come to Rome.

SERVANT

He did receive his letters, and is coming;
And bid me say to you by word of mouth —
O Cæsar! —

[*Seeing the body.*

ANTONY

Thy heart is big, get thee apart and weep.
Passion, I see, is catching; for mine eyes,
Seeing those beads of sorrow stand in thine,
Begin to water. Is thy master coming?

SERVANT

He lies to-night within seven leagues of Rome.

ANTONY

Post back with speed, and tell him what hath chanc'd:
Here is a mourning Rome, a dangerous Rome,
No Rome of safety for Octavius yet;
Hie hence, and tell him so. Yet, stay awhile;
Thou shalt not back till I have borne this corse
Into the market-place: there shall I try,
In my oration, how the people take
The cruel issue of these bloody men;
According to the which, thou shalt discourse
To young Octavius of the state of things.
Lend me your hand.

[*Exeunt with* CAESAR'S *body.*

SCENE II

The same. The Forum.

Enter BRUTUS *and* CASSIUS, *and a throng of*
CITIZENS.

CITIZENS

We will be satisfied; let us be satisfied

BRUTUS

Then follow me, and give me audience, friends.
Cassius, go you into the other street,
And part the numbers.
Those that will hear me speak, let 'em stay here;
Those that will follow Cassius, go with him;
And public reasons shall be rendered
Of Cæsar's death.

FIRST CITIZEN
     I will hear Brutus speak.

SECOND CITIZEN
I will hear Cassius; and compare their reasons,
When severally we hear them rendered.
  [*Exit* CASSIUS, *with some of the* CITIZENS. BRUTUS
           goes into the rostrum.

THIRD CITIZEN
The noble Brutus is ascended: silence!

BRUTUS
Be patient till the last.
Romans, countrymen, and lovers! hear me for my cause;
and be silent, that you may hear: believe me for mine
honour; and have respect to mine honour, that you may
believe: censure me in your wisdom; and awake your
senses, that you may the better judge. If there be any in
this assembly, any dear friend of Cæsar's, to him I say,
that Brutus' love to Cæsar was no less than his. If, then,
that friend demand why Brutus rose against Cæsar, this
is my answer, — Not that I loved Cæsar less, but that I
loved Rome more. Had you rather Cæsar were living,
and die all slaves, than that Cæsar were dead, to live all
free men? As Cæsar loved me, I weep for him; as he was
fortunate, I rejoice at it; as he was valiant, I honour him:
but, as he was ambitious, I slew him. There is tears for
his love; joy for his fortune; honour for his valour; and
death for his ambition. Who is here so base that would
be a bondman? If any, speak; for him have I offended.
Who is here so rude that would not be a Roman? If any,
speak; for him have I offended. Who is here so vile that
will not love his country? If any, speak; for him have I
offended. I pause for a reply.

CITIZENS
None, Brutus, none.

BRUTUS
Then none have I offended. I have done no more to
Cæsar than you shall do to Brutus. The question of his

BRUTUS Romans, countrymen, and lovers! hear me for my cause.

death is enroll'd in the Capitol; his glory not extenuated, wherein he was worthy; nor his offences enforced, for which he suffer'd death.

Enter ANTONY *and others, with* CAESAR'S *body.*

Here comes his body, mourn'd by Mark Antony: who,
though he had no hand in his death, shall receive the
benefit of his dying, a place in the commonwealth; as
which of you shall not? With this I depart, — that, as I
slew my best lover for the good of Rome, I have the same
dagger for myself, when it shall please my country to
need my death.

CITIZENS
  Live, Brutus! live, live!

FIRST CITIZEN
  Bring him with triumph home unto his house.

SECOND CITIZEN
  Give him a statue with his ancestors.

THIRD CITIZEN
  Let him be Cæsar.

FOURTH CITIZEN
                  Cæsar's better parts
  Shall be crown'd in Brutus.

FIRST CITIZEN
  We'll bring him to his house with shouts and clamours.

BRUTUS
  My countrymen, —

SECOND CITIZEN
                  Peace, silence! Brutus speaks.

FIRST CITIZEN
  Peace, ho!

BRUTUS
  Good countrymen, let me depart alone,
  And, for my sake, stay here with Antony:
  Do grace to Cæsar's corpse, and grace his speech
  Tending to Cæsar's glories; which Mark Antony,
  By our permission, is allow'd to make.
  I do entreat you, not a man depart,
  Save I alone, till Antony have spoke.

                                        [*Exit.*

FIRST CITIZEN
Stay, ho! and let us hear Mark Antony.

THIRD CITIZEN
Let him go up into the public chair;
We'll hear him. — Noble Antony, go up.

ANTONY
For Brutus' sake, I am beholding to you.

[*Ascends.*

FOURTH CITIZEN
What does he say of Brutus?

THIRD CITIZEN
     He says, for Brutus' sake,
He finds himself beholding to us all.

FOURTH CITIZEN
'Twere best he speak no harm of Brutus here.

FIRST CITIZEN
This Cæsar was a tyrant.

THIRD CITIZEN
     Nay, that's certain:
We are blest that Rome is rid of him.

SECOND CITIZEN
Peace! let us hear what Antony can say.

ANTONY
You gentle Romans, —

CITIZENS
     Peace, ho! let us hear him.

ANTONY
Friends, Romans, countrymen, lend me your ears;
I come to bury Cæsar, not to praise him.
The evil that men do lives after them;
The good is oft interred with their bones:
So let it be with Cæsar. The noble Brutus
Hath told you Cæsar was ambitious:
If it were so, it was a grievous fault;
And grievously hath Cæsar answer'd it.
Here, under leave of Brutus and the rest, —

For Brutus is an honourable man;
So are they all, all honourable men, —
Come I to speak in Cæsar's funeral.
He was my friend, faithful and just to me:
But Brutus says he was ambitious;
And Brutus is an honourable man.
He hath brought many captives home to Rome,
Whose ransoms did the general coffers fill:
Did this in Cæsar seem ambitious?
When that the poor have cried, Cæsar hath wept:
Ambition should be made of sterner stuff:
Yet Brutus says he was ambitious;
And Brutus is an honourable man.
You all did see that on the Lupercal
I thrice presented him a kingly crown,
Which he did thrice refuse: was this ambition?
Yet Brutus says he was ambitious;
And, sure, he is an honourable man.
I speak not to disprove what Brutus spoke,
But here I am to speak what I do know.
You all did love him once, — not without cause:
What cause withholds you, then, to mourn for him?
O judgement, thou art fled to brutish beasts,
And men have lost their reason! — Bear with me;
My heart is in the coffin there with Cæsar,
And I must pause till it come back to me.

FIRST CITIZEN
Methinks there is much reason in his sayings.

SECOND CITIZEN
If thou consider rightly of the matter,
Cæsar has had great wrong.

THIRD CITIZEN
      Has he, masters?
I fear there will a worse come in his place.

FOURTH CITIZEN
Mark'd ye his words? He would not take the crown;
Therefore 'tis certain he was not ambitious.

FIRST CITIZEN
  If it be found so, some will dear abide it.

SECOND CITIZEN
  Poor soul! his eyes are red as fire with weeping.

THIRD CITIZEN
  There's not a nobler man in Rome than Antony.

FOURTH CITIZEN
  Now mark him, he begins again to speak.

ANTONY
  But yesterday the word of Cæsar might
  Have stood against the world: now lies he there,
  And none so poor to do him reverence.
  O masters, if I were dispos'd to stir
  Your hearts and minds to mutiny and rage,
  I should do Brutus wrong, and Cassius wrong,
  Who, you all know, are honourable men:
  I will not do them wrong; I rather choose
  To wrong the dead, to wrong myself, and you,
  Than I will wrong such honourable men.
  But here's a parchment with the seal of Cæsar, —
  I found it in his closet, — 'tis his will:
  Let but the commons hear this testament, —
  Which, pardon me, I do not mean to read, —
  And they would go and kiss dead Cæsar's wounds,
  And dip their napkins in his sacred blood;
  Yea, beg a hair of him for memory,
  And, dying, mention it within their wills,
  Bequeathing it, as a rich legacy,
  Unto their issue.

FOURTH CITIZEN
  We'll hear the will: read it, Mark Antony.

CITIZENS
  The will, the will! we will hear Cæsar's will.

ANTONY
  Have patience, gentle friends, I must not read it;
  It is not meet you know how Cæsar lov'd you.
  You are not wood, you are not stones, but men;

And, being men, hearing the will of Cæsar,
It will inflame you, it will make you mad:
'Tis good you know not that you are his heirs;
For, if you should, O, what would come of it!

FOURTH CITIZEN
Read the will: we'll hear it, Antony;
You shall read us the will, — Cæsar's will.

ANTONY
Will you be patient? will you stay awhile?
I have o'ershot myself to tell you of it:
I fear I wrong the honourable men
Whose daggers have stabb'd Cæsar; I do fear it.

FOURTH CITIZEN
They were traitors: honourable men!

CITIZENS
The will! the testament!

SECOND CITIZEN
They were villains, murderers: the will! read the will.

ANTONY
You will compel me, then, to read the will?
Then make a ring about the corpse of Cæsar,
And let me show you him that made the will.
Shall I descend? and will you give me leave?

CITIZENS
Come down.

SECOND CITIZEN
Descend.

THIRD CITIZEN
You shall have leave.

[ANTONY *descends.*

FOURTH CITIZEN
A ring; stand round.

FIRST CITIZEN
Stand from the hearse, stand from the body.

SECOND CITIZEN
Room for Antony, — most noble Antony.

ANTONY

Nay, press not so upon me; stand far off.

CITIZENS

Stand back; room; bear back.

ANTONY

If you have tears, prepare to shed them now.
You all do know this mantle: I remember
The first time ever Cæsar put it on;
'Twas on a summer's evening, in his tent,
That day he overcame the Nervii: —
Look, in this place ran Cassius' dagger through:
See what a rent the envious Casca made:
Through this the well-beloved Brutus stabb'd;
And, as he pluck'd his cursed steel away,
Mark how the blood of Cæsar follow'd it,
As rushing out of doors, to be resolved
If Brutus so unkindly knock'd, or no;
For Brutus, as you know, was Cæsar's angel:
Judge, O you gods, how dearly Cæsar lov'd him!
This was the most unkindest cut of all;
For when the noble Cæsar saw him stab,
Ingratitude, more strong than traitors' arms,
Quite vanquish'd him: then burst his mighty heart;
And, in his mantle muffling up his face,
Even at the base of Pompey's statua,
Which all the while ran blood, great Cæsar fell.
O, what a fall was there, my countrymen!
Then I, and you, and all of us fell down,
Whilst bloody treason flourish'd over us.
O, now you weep; and, I perceive, you feel
The dint of pity: these are gracious drops.
Kind souls, what, weep you when you but behold
Our Cæsar's vesture wounded? Look you here,
Here is himself, marr'd, as you see, with traitors.

FIRST CITIZEN

O piteous spectacle!

SECOND CITIZEN
  O noble Cæsar!

THIRD CITIZEN
  O woeful day!

FOURTH CITIZEN
  O traitors, villains!

FIRST CITIZEN
  O most bloody sight!

SECOND CITIZEN
  We will be revenged.

CITIZENS
  Revenge, — about, — seek, — burn, — fire, — kill, —
  slay, — let not a traitor live!

ANTONY
  Stay, countrymen.

FIRST CITIZEN
  Peace there! hear the noble Antony.

SECOND CITIZEN
  We'll hear him, we'll follow him, we'll die with him.

ANTONY
  Good friends, sweet friends, let me not stir you up
  To such a sudden flood of mutiny.
  They that have done this deed are honourable; —
  What private griefs they have, alas, I know not,
  That made them do it; — they are wise and honourable,
  And will, no doubt, with reasons answer you.
  I come not, friends, to steal away your hearts:
  I am no orator, as Brutus is;
  But, as you know me all, a plain blunt man,
  That love my friend; and that they know full well
  That gave me public leave to speak of him:
  For I have neither wit, nor words, nor worth,
  Action, nor utterance, nor the power of speech,
  To stir men's blood: I only speak right on;
  I tell you that which you yourselves do know;

Show you sweet Cæsar's wounds, poor poor dumb
   mouths,
And bid them speak for me: but were I Brutus,
And Brutus Antony, there were an Antony
Would ruffle up your spirits, and put a tongue
In every wound of Cæsar, that should move
The stones of Rome to rise and mutiny.

CITIZENS

We'll mutiny.

FIRST CITIZEN

We'll burn the house of Brutus.

THIRD CITIZEN

Away, then! come, seek the conspirators.

ANTONY

Yet hear me, countrymen; yet hear me speak.

CITIZENS

Peace, ho! hear Antony, — most noble Antony.

ANTONY

Why, friends, you go to do you know not what:
Wherein hath Cæsar thus deserv'd your loves?
Alas, you know not, — I must tell you, then: —
You have forgot the will I told you of.

CITIZENS

Most true; the will: — let's stay and hear the will.

ANTONY

Here is the will, and under Cæsar's seal: —
To every Roman citizen he gives,
To every several man, seventy-five drachmas.

SECOND CITIZEN

Most noble Cæsar! — we'll revenge his death.

THIRD CITIZEN

O royal Cæsar!

ANTONY

Hear me with patience.

CITIZENS

Peace, ho!

ANTONY

Moreover, he hath left you all his walks,
His private arbours, and new-planted orchards,
On this side Tiber; he hath left them you,
And to your heirs for ever, — common pleasures,
To walk abroad, and recreate yourselves.
Here was a Cæsar! when comes such another?

FIRST CITIZEN

Never, never. — Come, away, away!
We'll burn his body in the holy place,
And with the brands fire the traitors' houses.
Take up the body.

SECOND CITIZEN

Go fetch fire.

THIRD CITIZEN

Pluck down benches.

FOURTH CITIZEN

Pluck down forms, windows, any thing.

[*Exeunt* CITIZENS *with the body.*

ANTONY

Now let it work: — mischief, thou art afoot,
Take thou what course thou wilt!

Enter SERVANT.

How now, fellow!

SERVANT

Sir, Octavius is already come to Rome.

ANTONY

Where is he?

SERVANT

He and Lepidus are at Cæsar's house.

ANTONY

And thither will I straight to visit him:
He comes upon a wish. Fortune is merry,
And in this mood will give us any thing.

SERVANT

I heard him say, Brutus and Cassius

Are rid like madmen through the gates of Rome.

ANTONY

Belike they had some notice of the people
How I had mov'd them. Bring me to Octavius. [*Exeunt.*

SCENE III

The same. A street.

Enter CINNA *the poet, and after him the* CITIZENS.

CINNA

I dreamt to-night that I did feast with Cæsar,
And things unlucky charge my fantasy:
I have no will to wander forth of doors,
Yet something leads me forth.

FIRST CITIZEN

What is your name?

SECOND CITIZEN

Whither are you going?

THIRD CITIZEN

Where do you dwell?

FOURTH CITIZEN

Are you a married man or a bachelor?

SECOND CITIZEN

Answer every man directly.

FIRST CITIZEN

Ay, and briefly.

FOURTH CITIZEN

Ay, and wisely.

THIRD CITIZEN

Ay, and truly, you were best.

CINNA

What is my name? Whither am I going? Where do I
dwell? Am I a married man or a bachelor? Then, to
answer every man directly and briefly, wisely and truly: —
wisely I say, I am a bachelor.

SECOND CITIZEN

That's as much as to say, they are fools that marry: —
you'll bear me a bang for that, I fear. Proceed; directly.

CINNA

Directly, I am going to Cæsar's funeral.

FIRST CITIZEN

As a friend or an enemy?

CINNA

As a friend.

SECOND CITIZEN

That matter is answer'd directly.

FOURTH CITIZEN

For your dwelling, — briefly.

CINNA

Briefly, I dwell by the Capitol.

THIRD CITIZEN

Your name, sir, truly.

CINNA

Truly, my name is Cinna.

FIRST CITIZEN

Tear him to pieces; he's a conspirator.

CINNA

I am Cinna the poet, I am Cinna the poet.

FOURTH CITIZEN

Tear him for his bad verses, tear him for his bad verses.

CINNA

I am not Cinna the conspirator.

FOURTH CITIZEN

It is no matter, his name's Cinna; pluck but his name
out of his heart, and turn him going.

THIRD CITIZEN

Tear him, tear him! Come, brands, ho! fire-brands: to
Brutus', to Cassius'; burn all: some to Decius' house,
and some to Casca's; some to Ligarius': away, go!

[*Exeunt.*

ACT IV

SCENE I

Rome. A room in ANTONY'S *house.*
ANTONY, OCTAVIUS, *and* LEPIDUS,
seated at a table.

ANTONY
These many, then, shall die; their names are prick'd.

OCTAVIUS
Your brother too must die; consent you, Lepidus?

LEPIDUS
I do consent, —

OCTAVIUS
          Prick him down, Antony.

LEPIDUS
Upon condition Publius shall not live,
Who is your sister's son, Mark Antony.

ANTONY

He shall not live; look, with a spot I damn him.
But, Lepidus, go you to Cæsar's house;
Fetch the will hither, and we shall determine
How to cut off some charge in legacies.

LEPIDUS

What, shall I find you here?

OCTAVIUS

Or here, or at
The Capitol.

[*Exit* LEPIDUS.

ANTONY

This is a slight unmeritable man,
Meet to be sent on errands: is it fit,
The threefold world divided, he should stand
One of the three to share it?

OCTAVIUS

So you thought him;
And took his voice who should be prick'd to die,
In our black sentence and proscription.

ANTONY

Octavius, I have seen more days than you:
And though we lay these honours on this man,
To ease ourselves of divers slanderous loads,
He shall but bear them as the ass bears gold,
To groan and sweat under the business,
Either led or driven, as we point the way;
And having brought our treasure where we will,
Then take we down his load, and turn him off,
Like to the empty ass, to shake his ears,
And graze in commons.

OCTAVIUS

You may do your will:
But he's a tried and valiant soldier.

ANTONY

So is my horse, Octavius; and for that
I do appoint him store of provender:

It is a creature that I teach to fight,
To wind, to stop, to run directly on, —
His corporal motion govern'd by my spirit.
And, in some taste, is Lepidus but so;
He must be taught, and train'd, and bid go forth: —
A barren-spirited fellow; one that feeds
On objects, arts, and imitations,
Which, out of use and stal'd by other men,
Begin his fashion: do not talk of him
But as a property. And now, Octavius,
Listen great things: — Brutus and Cassius
Are levying powers: we must straight make head:
Therefore let our alliance be combined,
Our best friends made, and our best means stretch'd out;
And let us presently go sit in council,
How covert matters may be best disclosed,
And open perils surest answered.

OCTAVIUS

Let us do so: for we are at the stake,
And bay'd about with many enemies;
And some that smile have in their hearts, I fear,
Millions of mischiefs.

[*Exeunt.*

SCENE II

Before BRUTUS' *tent, in the camp near Sardis.*

Drum. Enter BRUTUS, LUCILIUS, LUCIUS, *and the*
ARMY; TITINIUS *and* PINDARUS *meet them.*

BRUTUS

Stand, ho!

LUCILIUS

Give the word, ho! and stand.

BRUTUS

What now, Lucilius! is Cassius near?

LUCILIUS

He is at hand; and Pindarus is come
To do you salutation from his master.

BRUTUS

He greets me well. — Your master, Pindarus,
In his own change, or by ill officers,
Hath given me some worthy cause to wish
Things done, undone: but, if he be at hand
I shall be satisfied.

PINDARUS

          I do not doubt
But that my noble master will appear
Such as he is, full of regard and honour.

BRUTUS

He is not doubted. — A word, Lucilius;
How he receiv'd you, let me be resolv'd.

LUCILIUS

With courtesy and with respect enough;
But not with such familiar instances,
Nor with such free and friendly conference,
As he hath used of old.

BRUTUS

          Thou hast described
A hot friend cooling: ever note, Lucilius,
When love begins to sicken and decay,
It useth an enforced ceremony.
There are no tricks in plain and simple faith:
But hollow men, like horses hot at hand,
Make gallant show and promise of their mettle;
But when they should endure the bloody spur,
They fall their crests, and, like deceitful jades,
Sink in the trial. Comes his army on?

LUCILIUS

They mean this night in Sardis to be quarter'd;
The greater part, the horse in general,
Are come with Cassius.

                    [*March without.*

BRUTUS   Hark! he is arriv'd: —
March gently on to meet him.

Enter CASSIUS *and his* POWERS.

CASSIUS
Stand, ho!

BRUTUS
Stand, ho! Speak the word along.

FIRST SOLDIER
Stand!

SECOND SOLDIER
Stand!

THIRD SOLDIER
Stand!

CASSIUS
Most noble brother, you have done me wrong.

BRUTUS
Judge me, you gods! wrong I mine enemies?
And if not so, how should I wrong a brother?

CASSIUS
Brutus, this sober form of yours hides wrongs;
And when you do them —

BRUTUS
                    Cassius, be content;
Speak your griefs softly, — I do know you well: —
Before the eyes of both our armies here,
Which should perceive nothing but love from us,
Let us not wrangle: bid them move away;
Then in my tent, Cassius, enlarge your griefs,
And I will give you audience.

CASSIUS
                    Pindarus,
Bid our commanders lead their charges off
A little from this ground.

BRUTUS
Lucilius, do you the like; and let no man
Come to our tent till we have done our conference.
Let Lucius and Titinius guard our door.

                              [*Exeunt.*

SCENE III

Within the tent of BRUTUS.
Enter BRUTUS *and* CASSIUS.

CASSIUS

That you have wrong'd me doth appear in this:
You have condemn'd and noted Lucius Pella
For taking bribes here of the Sardians;
Wherein my letters, praying on his side,
Because I knew the man, were slighted off.

BRUTUS

You wrong'd yourself to write in such a case.

CASSIUS

In such a time as this it is not meet
That every nice offence should bear his comment.

BRUTUS

Let me tell you, Cassius, you yourself
Are much condemn'd to have an itching palm;
To sell and mart your offices for gold
To undeservers.

CASSIUS

     I an itching palm!
You know that you are Brutus that speak this,
Or, by the gods, this speech were else your last.

BRUTUS

The name of Cassius honours this corruption,
And chastisement doth therefore hide his head.

CASSIUS

Chastisement!

BRUTUS

Remember March, the ides of March remember:
Did not great Julius bleed for justice' sake?
What villain touch'd his body, that did stab,
And not for justice? What, shall one of us,
That struck the foremost man of all this world
But for supporting robbers, shall we now
Contaminate our fingers with base bribes,

And sell the mighty space of our large honours
For so much trash as may be grasped thus? —
I had rather be a dog, and bay the moon,
Than such a Roman.

CASSIUS

                    Brutus, bay not me, —
I'll not endure it: you forget yourself,
To hedge me in; I am a soldier, I,
Older in practice, abler than yourself
To make conditions.

BRUTUS

                    Go to; you are not, Cassius.

CASSIUS

I am.

BRUTUS

I say you are not.

CASSIUS

Urge me no more, I shall forget myself;
Have mind upon your health, tempt me no further.

BRUTUS

Away, slight man!

CASSIUS

Is't possible?

BRUTUS

                    Hear me, for I will speak.
Must I give way and room to your rash choler?
Shall I be frighted when a madman stares?

CASSIUS

O ye gods, ye gods! must I endure all this?

BRUTUS

All this! ay, more: fret till your proud heart break;
Go show your slaves how choleric you are,
And make your bondmen tremble. Must I budge?
Must I observe you? must I stand and crouch
Under your testy humour? By the gods,
You shall digest the venom of your spleen,
Though it do split you; for, from this day forth,

I'll use you for my mirth, yea, for my laughter,
When you are waspish.

CASSIUS

      Is it come to this?

BRUTUS

You say you are a better soldier:
Let it appear so; make your vaunting true,
And it shall please me well: for mine own part,
I shall be glad to learn of noble men.

CASSIUS

You wrong me every way; you wrong me, Brutus;
I said, an elder soldier, not a better:
Did I say 'better'?

BRUTUS

     If you did, I care not.

CASSIUS

When Cæsar liv'd, he durst not thus have mov'd me.

BRUTUS

Peace, peace! you durst not so have tempted him.

CASSIUS

I durst not!

BRUTUS

No.

CASSIUS

What, durst not tempt him!

BRUTUS

     For your life you durst not.

CASSIUS

Do not presume too much upon my love;
I may do that I shall be sorry for.

BRUTUS

You have done that you should be sorry for.
There is no terror, Cassius, in your threats;
For I am arm'd so strong in honesty,
That they pass by me as the idle wind,
Which I respect not. I did send to you

For certain sums of gold, which you denied me;
For I can raise no money by vile means:
By heaven, I had rather coin my heart,
And drop my blood for drachmas, than to wring
From the hard hands of peasants their vile trash
By any indirection; — I did send
To you for gold to pay my legions,
Which you denied me: was that done like Cassius?
Should I have answer'd Caius Cassius so?
When Marcus Brutus grows so covetous,
To lock such rascal counters from his friends,
Be ready, gods, with all your thunderbolts;
Dash him to pieces!

CASSIUS
               I denied you not.

BRUTUS
You did.

CASSIUS
I did not: — he was but a fool that brought
My answer back. — Brutus hath riv'd my heart:
A friend should bear his friend's infirmities,
But Brutus makes mine greater than they are.

BRUTUS
I do not, till you practise them on me.

CASSIUS
You love me not.

BRUTUS
            I do not like your faults.

CASSIUS
A friendly eye could never see such faults.

BRUTUS
A flatterer's would not, though they do appear
As huge as high Olympus.

CASSIUS
Come, Antony, and young Octavius, come,
Revenge yourselves alone on Cassius,
For Cassius is a-weary of the world;

Hated by one he loves; brav'd by his brother;
Check'd like a bondman; all his faults observed,
Set in a note-book, learn'd, and conn'd by rote,
To cast into my teeth. O, I could weep
My spirit from mine eyes! — There is my dagger,
And here my naked breast; within, a heart
Dearer than Pluto's mine, richer than gold:
If that thou be'st a Roman, take it forth;
I, that denied thee gold, will give my heart:
Strike, as thou didst at Cæsar; for, I know,
When thou didst hate him worst, thou lovedst him
    better
Than ever thou lovedst Cassius.

BRUTUS

                Sheathe your dagger:
Be angry when you will, it shall have scope;
Do what you will, dishonour shall be humour.
O Cassius, you are yoked with a lamb
That carries anger as the flint bears fire;
Who, much enforced, shows a hasty spark,
And straight is cold again.

CASSIUS

             Hath Cassius liv'd
To be but mirth and laughter to his Brutus,
When grief, and blood ill-temper'd, vexeth him?

BRUTUS

When I spoke that, I was ill-temper'd too.

CASSIUS

Do you confess so much? Give me your hand.

BRUTUS

And my heart too.

CASSIUS

        O Brutus, —

BRUTUS

                  What's the matter?

CASSIUS

Have not you love enough to bear with me,

When that rash humour which my mother gave me
Makes me forgetful?

BRUTUS

           Yes, Cassius; and, from henceforth,
When you are over-earnest with your Brutus,
He'll think your mother chides, and leave you so.

POET [*within*]

Let me go in to see the generals;
There is some grudge between 'em, 'tis not meet
They be alone.

LUCILIUS [*without*].

You shall not come to them.

POET [*without*].

Nothing but death shall stay me.

    Enter POET, *follow'd by* LUCILIUS,
        TITINIUS, *and* LUCIUS.

CASSIUS

How now! what's the matter?

POET

For shame, you generals! what do you mean?
Love, and be friends, as two such men should be;
For I have seen more years, I'm sure, than ye.

CASSIUS

Ha, ha! how vilely doth this cynic rime!

BRUTUS

Get you hence, sirrah; saucy fellow, hence!

CASSIUS

Bear with him, Brutus; 'tis his fashion.

BRUTUS

I'll know his humour, when he knows his time:
What should the wars do with these jigging fools? —
Companion, hence!

CASSIUS

        Away, away, be gone!

                       [*Exit* POET.

BRUTUS

Lucilius and Titinius, bid the commanders
Prepare to lodge their companies to-night.

CASSIUS

And come yourselves, and bring Messala with you
Immediately to us.

              [Exeunt LUCILIUS *and* TITINIUS.

BRUTUS

          Lucius, a bowl of wine!

CASSIUS

I did not think you could have been so angry.

BRUTUS

O Cassius, I am sick of many griefs.

CASSIUS

Of your philosophy you make no use,
If you give place to accidental evils.

BRUTUS

No man bears sorrow better: — Portia is dead.

CASSIUS

Ha! Portia!

BRUTUS

She is dead.

CASSIUS

How scap'd I killing when I cross'd you so? —
O insupportable and touching loss! —
Upon what sickness?

BRUTUS

          Impatient of my absence,
And grief that young Octavius with Mark Antony
Have made themselves so strong; — for with her
    death
That tidings came; — with this she fell distract,
And, her attendants absent, swallow'd fire.

CASSIUS

And died so?

BRUTUS
  Even so.

CASSIUS
                    O ye immortal gods!
          Enter LUCIUS, *with wine and taper.*

BRUTUS
  Speak no more of her. — Give me a bowl of wine. —
  In this I bury all unkindness, Cassius.

                                              [*Drinks.*

CASSIUS
  My heart is thirsty for that noble pledge. —
  Fill, Lucius, till the wine o'erswell the cup;
  I cannot drink too much of Brutus' love.

                                              [*Drinks.*

BRUTUS
  Come in, Titinius!

          Re-enter TITINIUS, *with* MESSALA.

                    Welcome, good Messala. —
  Now sit we close about this taper here,
  And call in question our necessities.

CASSIUS
  Portia, art thou gone?

BRUTUS
                    No more, I pray you. —
  Messala, I have here received letters,
  That young Octavius and Mark Antony
  Come down upon us with a mighty power,
  Bending their expedition toward Philippi.

MESSALA
  Myself have letters of the selfsame tenour.

BRUTUS
  With what addition?

MESSALA
  That by proscription and bills of outlawry,
  Octavius, Antony, and Lepidus
  Have put to death an hundred senators.

BRUTUS

Therein our letters do not well agree;
Mine speak of seventy senators that died
By their proscriptions, Cicero being one.

CASSIUS

Cicero one!

MESSALA

Cicero is dead,
And by that order of proscription. —
Had you your letters from your wife, my lord?

BRUTUS

No, Messala.

MESSALA

Nor nothing in your letters writ of her?

BRUTUS

Nothing, Messala.

MESSALA

That, methinks, is strange.

BRUTUS

Why ask you? hear you aught of her in yours?

MESSALA

No, my lord.

BRUTUS

Now, as you are a Roman, tell me true.

MESSALA

Then like a Roman bear the truth I tell:
For certain she is dead, and by strange manner.

BRUTUS

Why, farewell, Portia. — We must die, Messala:
With meditating that she must die once,
I have the patience to endure it now.

MESSALA

Even so great men great losses should endure.

CASSIUS

I have as much of this in art as you,
But yet my nature could not bear it so.

BRUTUS

Well, to our work alive. What do you think
Of marching to Philippi presently?

CASSIUS

I do not think it good.

BRUTUS

Your reason?

CASSIUS

This it is: —
'Tis better that the enemy seek us:
So shall he waste his means, weary his soldiers,
Doing himself offence; whilst we, lying still,
Are full of rest, defence, and nimbleness.

BRUTUS

Good reasons must, of force, give place to better.
The people 'twixt Philippi and this ground
Do stand but in a forc'd affection;
For they have grudg'd us contribution:
The enemy, marching along by them,
By them shall make a fuller number up,
Come on refresh'd, new-added, and encourag'd;
From which advantage shall we cut him off,
If at Philippi we do face him there,
These people at our back.

CASSIUS

Hear me, good brother.

BRUTUS

Under your pardon. — You must note beside,
That we have tried the utmost of our friends,
Our legions are brim-full, our cause is ripe:
The enemy increaseth every day;
We, at the height, are ready to decline.
There is a tide in the affairs of men,
Which, taken at the flood, leads on to fortune;
Omitted, all the voyage of their life
Is bound in shallows and in miseries.
On such a full sea are we now afloat;

And we must take the current when it serves,
Or lose our ventures.

CASSIUS

              Then, with your will, go on;
We'll along ourselves, and meet them at Philippi.

BRUTUS

The deep of night is crept upon our talk,
And nature must obey necessity;
Which we will niggard with a little rest.
There is no more to say?

CASSIUS

            No more. Good night:
Early to-morrow will we rise, and hence.

BRUTUS

Lucius, my gown! — Farewell, good Messala: —
Good night, Titinius: — noble, noble Cassius,
Good night, and good repose.

CASSIUS

            O my dear brother!
This was an ill beginning of the night:
Never come such division 'tween our souls!
Let it not, Brutus.

BRUTUS

            Every thing is well.

CASSIUS

Good night, my lord.

BRUTUS

            Good night, good brother.

TITINIUS and MESSALA

Good night, Lord Brutus.

BRUTUS

            Farewell, every one.

[*Exeunt* CASSIUS, TITINIUS, *and* MESSALA.
Re-enter LUCIUS, *with the gown.*

Give me the gown. Where is thy instrument?

LUCIUS

Here in the tent.

BRUTUS

What, thou speak'st drowsily?
Poor knave, I blame thee not; thou art o'er-watch'd.
Call Claudius and some other of my men;
I'll have them sleep on cushions in my tent.

LUCIUS

Varro and Claudius!

Enter VARRO *and* CLAUDIUS.

VARRO

Calls my lord?

BRUTUS

I pray you, sirs, lie in my tent and sleep;
It may be I shall raise you by and by
On business to my brother Cassius.

VARRO

So please you, we will stand and watch your pleasure.

BRUTUS

I will not have it so: lie down, good sirs;
It may be I shall otherwise bethink me. —
Look, Lucius, here's the book I sought for so;
I put it in the pocket of my gown.

[VARRO *and* CLAUDIUS *lie down.*

LUCIUS

I was sure your lordship did not give it me.

BRUTUS

Bear with me, good boy, I am much forgetful.
Canst thou hold up thy heavy eyes awhile,
And touch thy instrument a strain or two?

LUCIUS

Ay, my lord, an't please you.

BRUTUS

It does, my boy:
I trouble thee too much, but thou art willing.

LUCIUS

  It is my duty, sir.

BRUTUS

  I should not urge thy duty past thy might;
  I know young bloods look for a time of rest.

LUCIUS

  I have slept, my lord, already.

BRUTUS

  It was well done; and thou shalt sleep again;
  I will not hold thee long: if I do live,
  I will be good to thee.

                              [*Music, and a song.*

  This is a sleepy tune: — O murderous slumber,
  Lay'st thou thy leaden mace upon my boy,
  That plays thee music? — Gentle knave, good night:
  I will not do thee so much wrong to wake thee:
  If thou dost nod, thou break'st thy instrument;
  I'll take it from thee; and, good boy, good night. —
  Let me see, let me see; — is not the leaf turn'd down
  Where I left reading? Here it is, I think.

            Enter the GHOST OF CAESAR.

  How ill this taper burns! — Ha! who comes here?
  I think it is the weakness of mine eyes
  That shapes this monstrous apparition.
  It comes upon me. — Art thou any thing?
  Art thou some god, some angel, or some devil,
  That makest my blood cold, and my hair to stare?
  Speak to me what thou art.

GHOST OF CAESAR

  Thy evil spirit, Brutus.

BRUTUS

                        Why comest thou?

GHOST OF CAESAR

  To tell thee thou shalt see me at Philippi.

BRUTUS

  Well; then I shall see thee again?

GHOST OF CAESAR
Ay, at Philippi.

BRUTUS
Why, I will see thee at Philippi, then.

[GHOST *vanishes.*

Now I have taken heart thou vanishest:
Ill spirit, I would hold more talk with thee. —
Boy, Lucius! — Varro! Claudius! — Sirs, awake! —
Claudius!

LUCIUS
The strings, my lord, are false.

BRUTUS
He thinks he still is at his instrument. —
Lucius, awake!

LUCIUS
My lord?

BRUTUS
Didst thou dream, Lucius, that thou so criedst out?

LUCIUS
My lord, I do not know that I did cry.

BRUTUS
Yes, that thou didst: didst thou see any thing?

LUCIUS
Nothing, my lord.

BRUTUS
Sleep again, Lucius. — Sirrah, Claudius! —
[*to* VARRO] Fellow thou, awake!

VARRO
My lord?

CLAUDIUS
My lord?

BRUTUS
Why did you so cry out, sirs, in your sleep?

VARRO *and* **CLAUDIUS**
Did we, my lord?

BRUTUS
    Ay: saw you any thing?

VARRO
 No, my lord, I saw nothing.

CLAUDIUS
    Nor I, my lord.

BRUTUS
 Go and commend me to my brother Cassius;
 Bid him set on his powers betimes before,
 And we will follow.

VARRO and **CLAUDIUS**
    It shall be done, my lord.   [*Exeunt.*

ACT V

SCENE I

The plains of Philippi.
Enter OCTAVIUS, ANTONY, *and their* ARMY.

OCTAVIUS
 Now, Antony, our hopes are answered:
 You said the enemy would not come down,
 But keep the hills and upper regions:
 It proves not so; their battles are at hand;
 They mean to warn us at Philippi here,
 Answering before we do demand of them.

ANTONY
 Tut, I am in their bosoms, and I know
 Wherefore they do it: they could be content
 To visit other places; and come down
 With fearful bravery, thinking by this face
 To fasten in our thoughts that they have courage;
 But 'tis not so.

    Enter a MESSENGER.

MESSENGER
            Prepare you, generals:
The enemy comes on in gallant show;
Their bloody sign of battle is hung out,
And something to be done immediately.

ANTONY
  Octavius, lead your battle softly on,
Upon the left hand of the even field.

OCTAVIUS
  Upon the right hand I; keep thou the left.

ANTONY
  Why do you cross me in this exigent?

OCTAVIUS
  I do not cross you; but I will do so.

                                        [*March.*

  Drum. Enter BRUTUS, CASSIUS, *and their* ARMY;
    LUCILIUS, TITINIUS, MESSALA, *and others.*

BRUTUS
  They stand, and would have parley.

CASSIUS
  Stand fast, Titinius: we must out and talk.

OCTAVIUS
  Mark Antony, shall we give sign of battle?

ANTONY

No, Cæsar, we will answer on their charge.
Make forth; the generals would have some words.

OCTAVIUS

Stir not until the signal.

BRUTUS

Words before blows: — is it so, countrymen?

OCTAVIUS

Not that we love words better, as you do.

BRUTUS

Good words are better than bad strokes, Octavius.

ANTONY

In your bad strokes, Brutus, you give good words;
Witness the hole you made in Cæsar's heart,
Crying, 'Long live! hail, Cæsar!'

CASSIUS

                Antony,
The posture of your blows are yet unknown;
But for your words, they rob the Hybla bees,
And leave them honeyless.

ANTONY

                Not stingless too.

BRUTUS

O, yes, and soundless, too;
For you have stol'n their buzzing, Antony,
And very wisely threat before you sting.

ANTONY

Villains, you did not so, when your vile daggers
Hack'd one another in the sides of Cæsar:
You show'd your teeth like apes, and fawn'd like
    hounds,
And bow'd like bondmen, kissing Cæsar's feet;
Whilst damned Casca, like a cur, behind
Struck Cæsar on the neck. O you flatterers!

CASSIUS

Flatterers! — Now, Brutus, thank yourself:
This tongue had not offended so to-day,

If Cassius might have rul'd.

OCTAVIUS

Come, come, the cause: if arguing make us sweat,
The proof of it will turn to redder drops.
Look, —
I draw a sword against conspirators;
When think you that the sword goes up again? —
Never, till Cæsar's three-and-thirty wounds
Be well avenged; or till another Cæsar
Have added slaughter to the words of traitors.

BRUTUS

Cæsar, thou canst not die by traitors' hands,
Unless thou bring'st them with thee.

OCTAVIUS

                    So I hope;
I was not born to die on Brutus' sword.

BRUTUS

O, if thou wert the noblest of thy strain,
Young man, thou couldst not die more honourable.

CASSIUS

A peevish schoolboy, worthless of such honour,
Join'd with a masker and a reveller!

ANTONY

Old Cassius still!

OCTAVIUS

              Come, Antony; away! —
Defiance, traitors, hurl we in your teeth:
If you dare fight to-day, come to the field;
If not, when you have stomachs.
        [*Exeunt* OCTAVIUS, ANTONY, *and their* ARMY.

CASSIUS

Why, now, blow wind, swell billow, and swim bark!
The storm is up, and all is on the hazard.

BRUTUS

Ho,
Lucilius! hark; a word with you.

LUCILIUS

My lord?
[BRUTUS *and* LUCILIUS *converse apart.*

CASSIUS
Messala, —

MESSALA
What says my general?

CASSIUS
Messala,
This is my birthday; as this very day
Was Cassius born. Give me thy hand, Messala:
Be thou my witness that, against my will,
As Pompey was, am I compell'd to set
Upon one battle all our liberties.
You know that I held Epicurus strong,
And his opinion: now I change my mind,
And partly credit things that do presage.
Coming from Sardis, on our former ensign
Two mighty eagles fell; and there they perch'd,
Gorging and feeding from our soldiers' hands;
Who to Philippi here consorted us:
This morning are they fled away and gone;
And in their steads do ravens, crows, and kites,
Fly o'er our heads, and downward look on us,
As we were sickly prey: their shadows seem
A canopy most fatal, under which
Our army lies, ready to give up the ghost.

MESSALA
Believe not so.

CASSIUS
I but believe it partly;
For I am fresh of spirit, and resolved
To meet all perils very constantly.

BRUTUS
Even so, Lucilius.

CASSIUS
Now, most noble Brutus,

The gods to-day stand friendly, that we may,
Lovers in peace, lead on our days to age!
But, since the affairs of men rest still incertain,
Let's reason with the worst that may befall.
If we do lose this battle, then is this
The very last time we shall speak together:
What are you, then, determined to do?

BRUTUS

Even by the rule of that philosophy
By which I did blame Cato for the death
Which he did give himself: — I know not how,
But I do find it cowardly and vile,
For fear of what might fall, so to prevent
The time of life: — arming myself with patience
To stay the providence of some high powers
That govern us below.

CASSIUS

     Then, if we lose this battle,
You are contented to be led in triumph
Through the streets of Rome?

BRUTUS

No, Cassius, no: think not, thou noble Roman,
That ever Brutus will go bound to Rome;
He bears too great a mind. But this same day
Must end that work the ides of March begun;
And whether we shall meet again I know not.
Therefore our everlasting farewell take: —
For ever, and for ever, farewell, Cassius!
If we do meet again, why, we shall smile;
If not, why, then, this parting was well made.

CASSIUS

For ever, and for ever, farewell, Brutus!
If we do meet again, we'll smile indeed;
If not, 'tis true this parting was well made.

BRUTUS

Why, then, lead on. — O, that a man might know
The end of this day's business ere it come!

But it sufficeth that the day will end,
And then the end is known. — Come, ho! away!

[*Exeunt.*

SCENE II

The same. The field of battle.

Alarums. Enter BRUTUS *and* MESSALA.

BRUTUS

Ride, ride, Messala, ride, and give these bills
Unto the legions on the other side:
Let them set on at once; for I perceive
But cold demeanour in Octavius' wing,
And sudden push gives them the overthrow.
Ride, ride, Messala: let them all come down.

[*Exeunt.*

SCENE III

The same. Another part of the field.

Alarums. Enter CASSIUS *and* TITINIUS.

CASSIUS

O look, Titinius, look, the villains fly!
Myself have to mine own turn'd enemy:
This ensign here of mine was turning back;
I slew the coward, and did take it from him.

TITINIUS

O Cassius, Brutus gave the word too early;
Who, having some advantage on Octavius,
Took it too eagerly: his soldiers fell to spoil,
Whilst we by Antony are all enclosed.

Enter PINDARUS.

PINDARUS

Fly further off, my lord, fly further off;
Mark Antony is in your tents, my lord:
Fly, therefore, noble Cassius, fly far off.

CASSIUS
This hill is far enough. — Look, look, Titinius;
Are those my tents where I perceive the fire?

TITINIUS
They are, my lord.

CASSIUS
Titinius, if thou lov'st me,
Mount thou my horse, and hide thy spurs in him,
Till he have brought thee up to yonder troops,
And here again; that I may rest assured
Whether yond troops are friend or enemy.

TITINIUS
I will be here again, even with a thought.

[*Exit.*

CASSIUS
Go, Pindarus, get higher on that hill;
My sight was ever thick; regard Titinius,
And tell me what thou notest about the field. —

[PINDARUS *goes up.*

This day I breathed first: time is come round,
And where I did begin, there shall I end;
My life is run his compass. — Sirrah, what news?

PINDARUS [*above*].
O my lord!

CASSIUS
What news?

PINDARUS [*above*].
Titinius is enclosed round about
With horsemen, that make to him on the spur; —
Yet he spurs on. — Now they are almost on him; —
Now, Titinius! —
Now some light: O, he lights too: he's ta'en; [*shout*] and,
    hark!
They shout for joy.

CASSIUS
                    Come down, behold no more. —
O, coward that I am, to live so long,

99

CASSIUS Come down, behold no more.

To see my best friend ta'en before my face!

PINDARUS *descends.*
Come hither, sirrah:
In Parthia did I take thee prisoner;
And then I swore thee, saving of thy life,
That whatsoever I did bid thee do,
Thou shouldst attempt it. Come now, keep thine oath;
Now be a freeman; and, with this good sword,

That ran through Cæsar's bowels, search this bosom.
Stand not to answer: here, take thou the hilts;
And, when my face is cover'd, as 'tis now,
Guide thou the sword. — Cæsar, thou art revenged,
Even with the sword that kill'd thee.

[*Dies.*

PINDARUS

So, I am free; yet would not so have been,
Durst I have done my will. O Cassius!
Far from this country Pindarus shall run,
Where never Roman shall take note of him.

[*Exit.*

Enter TITINIUS *with* MESSALA.

MESSALA

It is but change, Titinius; for Octavius
Is overthrown by noble Brutus' power,
As Cassius' legions are by Antony.

TITINIUS

These tidings will well comfort Cassius.

MESSALA

Where did you leave him?

TITINIUS

     All disconsolate,
With Pindarus his bondman, on this hill.

MESSALA

Is not that he that lies upon the ground?

TITINIUS

He lies not like the living. O my heart!

MESSALA

Is not that he?

TITINIUS

    No, this was he, Messala,
But Cassius is no more. — O setting sun,
As in thy red rays thou dost sink to night,
So in his red blood Cassius' day is set, —
The sun of Rome is set! Our day is gone;
Clouds, dews, and dangers come; our deeds are done!

Mistrust of my success hath done this deed.

MESSALA

Mistrust of good success hath done this deed.
O hateful Error, Melancholy's child,
Why dost thou show to the apt thoughts of men
The things that are not? O Error, soon conceived,
Thou never comest unto a happy birth,
But kill'st the mother that engender'd thee!

TITINIUS

What, Pindarus! where art thou, Pindarus?

MESSALA

Seek him, Titinius, whilst I go to meet
The noble Brutus, thrusting this report
Into his ears: I may say, thrusting it;
For piercing steel, and darts envenomed,
Shall be as welcome to the ears of Brutus
As tidings of this sight.

TITINIUS

              Hie you, Messala,
And I will seek for Pindarus the while.

                         [*Exit* MESSALA.

Why didst thou send me forth, brave Cassius?
Did I not meet thy friends? and did not they
Put on my brows this wreath of victory,
And bid me give it thee? Didst thou not hear their
    shouts?
Alas, thou hast misconstrued every thing!
But, hold thee, take this garland on thy brow;
Thy Brutus bid me give it thee, and I
Will do his bidding. — Brutus, come apace,
And see how I regarded Caius Cassius. —
By your leave, gods: — this is a Roman's part:
Come, Cassius' sword, and find Titinius' heart.

                              [*Dies.*

    Alarums. Enter MESSALA, *with* BRUTUS, *young*
CATO, STRATO, VOLUMNIUS, *and* LUCILIUS.

BRUTUS

Where, where, Messala, doth his body lie?

MESSALA

Lo, yonder; and Titinius mourning it.

BRUTUS

Titinius' face is upward.

YOUNG CATO

               He is slain.

BRUTUS

O Julius Cæsar, thou art mighty yet!
Thy spirit walks abroad, and turns our swords
In our own proper entrails.

                              [Low alarums.

YOUNG CATO

              Brave Titinius!
Look, whe'r he have not crown'd dead Cassius!

BRUTUS

Are yet two Romans living such as these? —
The last of all the Romans, fare thee well!
It is impossible that ever Rome
Should breed thy fellow. — Friends, I owe more tears
To this dead man than you shall see me pay. —
I shall find time, Cassius, I shall find time. —
Come, therefore, and to Thasos send his body:
His funerals shall not be in our camp,
Lest it discomfort us. — Lucilius, come; —
And come, young Cato; — let us to the field. —
Labeo and Flavius, set our battles on: —
'Tis three o'clock; and, Romans, yet ere night
We shall try fortune in a second fight.

                              [Exeunt.

SCENE IV

The same. Another part of the field.

Alarum. Enter, fighting, SOLDIERS *of both armies; then*
BRUTUS, YOUNG CATO, LUCILIUS, *and others.*

BRUTUS

Yet, countrymen, O, yet hold up your heads!

YOUNG CATO

What bastard doth not? Who will go with me?
I will proclaim my name about the field: —
I am the son of Marcus Cato, ho!
A foe to tyrants, and my country's friend;
I am the son of Marcus Cato, ho!

BRUTUS

And I am Brutus, Marcus Brutus, I;
Brutus, my country's friend; know me for Brutus!

[*Exit.*

LUCILIUS

O young and noble Cato, art thou down?
Why, now thou diest as bravely as Titinius;
And mayst be honour'd, being Cato's son.

FIRST SOLDIER

Yield, or thou diest.

LUCILIUS

Only I yield to die:
There is so much that thou wilt kill me straight;

[*Offering money.*

Kill Brutus, and be honour'd in his death.

FIRST SOLDIER

We must not. — A noble prisoner!

SECOND SOLDIER

Room, ho! Tell Antony, Brutus is ta'en.

FIRST SOLDIER

I'll tell the news: — here comes the general.

Enter ANTONY.

Brutus is ta'en, Brutus is ta'en, my lord.

ANTONY

Where is he?

LUCILIUS

Safe, Antony; Brutus is safe enough:
I dare assure thee that no enemy

Shall ever take alive the noble Brutus:
The gods defend him from so great a shame!
When you do find him, or alive or dead,
He will be found like Brutus, like himself.

ANTONY

This is not Brutus, friend; but, I assure you,
A prize no less in worth: keep this man safe,
Give him all kindness: I had rather have
Such men my friends than enemies. Go on,
And see whe'r Brutus be alive or dead:
And bring us word unto Octavius' tent
How every thing is chanced.

[*Exeunt.*

SCENE V

The same. Another part of the field.

Enter BRUTUS, DARDANIUS, CLITUS, STRATO,
and VOLUMNIUS.

BRUTUS

Come, poor remains of friends, rest on this rock.

CLITUS

Statilius show'd the torch-light; but, my lord,
He came not back: he is or ta'en or slain.

BRUTUS

Sit thee down, Clitus: slaying is the word;
It is a deed in fashion. Hark thee, Clitus.

[*Whispering.*

CLITUS

What, I, my lord? No, not for all the world.

BRUTUS

Peace, then, no words.

CLITUS

I'll rather kill myself.

BRUTUS

Hark thee, Dardanius.

[Whispers him.

DARDANIUS

            Shall I do such a deed?

CLITUS

  O Dardanius!

DARDANIUS

  O Clitus!

CLITUS

  What ill request did Brutus make to thee?

DARDANIUS

  To kill him, Clitus. Look, he meditates.

CLITUS

  Now is that noble vessel full of grief,
  That it runs over even at his eyes.

BRUTUS

  Come hither, good Volumnius; list a word.

VOLUMNIUS

  What says my lord?

BRUTUS

            Why, this, Volumnius:
  The ghost of Cæsar hath appear'd to me
  Two several times by night, — at Sardis once,
  And, this last night, here in Philippi fields:
  I know my hour is come.

VOLUMNIUS

            Not so, my lord.

BRUTUS

  Nay, I am sure it is, Volumnius.
  Thou seest the world, Volumnius, how it goes;
  Our enemies have beat us to the pit:

                [Loud alarums.

  It is more worthy to leap in ourselves,
  Than tarry till they push us. Good Volumnius,
  Thou know'st that we two went to school together;
  Even for that our love of old, I prithee,
  Hold thou my sword-hilts, whilst I run on it.

VOLUMNIUS

That's not an office for a friend, my lord.

[*Alarum still.*

CLITUS

Fly, fly, my lord; there is no tarrying here.

BRUTUS

Farewell to you; — and you; — and you, Volumnius. —
Strato, thou hast been all this while asleep;
Farewell to thee too, Strato. — Countrymen,
My heart doth joy, that yet, in all my life,
I found no man but he was true to me.
I shall have glory by this losing day,
More than Octavius and Mark Antony
By this vile conquest shall attain unto.
So, fare you well at once; for Brutus' tongue
Hath almost ended his life's history:
Night hangs upon mine eyes; my bones would rest,
That have but labour'd to attain this hour.

[*Alarums. Cry within,* 'Fly, fly, fly!'

CLITUS

Fly, my lord, fly.

BRUTUS

Hence! I will follow.

   [*Exeunt* CLITUS, DARDANIUS, *and* VOLUMNIUS.
I prithee, Strato, stay thou by thy lord:
Thou art a fellow of a good respect;
Thy life hath had some smatch of honour in it:
Hold, then, my sword, and turn away thy face,
While I do run upon it. Wilt thou, Strato?

STRATO

Give me your hand first: fare you well, my lord.

BRUTUS

Farewell, good Strato. — Cæsar, now be still:
I kill'd not thee with half so good a will.

[*He runs on his sword, and dies.*

Alarums. Retreat. Enter OCTAVIUS, ANTONY,
MESSALA, LUCILIUS, *and the* ARMY.

OCTAVIUS
What man is that?

MESSALA
My master's man. — Strato, where is thy master?

STRATO
Free from the bondage you are in, Messala:
The conquerors can but make a fire of him;
For Brutus only overcame himself,
And no man else hath honour by his death.

LUCILIUS
So Brutus should be found. — I thank thee, Brutus,
That thou hast prov'd Lucilius' saying true.

OCTAVIUS
All that serv'd Brutus, I will entertain them. —
Fellow, wilt thou bestow thy time with me?

STRATO
Ay, if Messala will prefer me to you.

OCTAVIUS
Do so, good Messala.

MESSALA
How died my master, Strato?

STRATO
I held the sword, and he did run on it.

MESSALA
Octavius, then take him to follow thee,
That did the latest service to my master.

ANTONY
This was the noblest Roman of them all:
All the conspirators, save only he,
Did that they did in envy of great Cæsar;
He only, in a general honest thought,
And common good to all, made one of them.
His life was gentle; and the elements
So mix'd in him, that Nature might stand up
And say to all the world, 'This was a man!'

OCTAVIUS

According to his virtue let us use him,
With all respect and rites of bur ial.
Within my tent his bones to-night shall lie,
Most like a soldier, order'd honourably. —
So, call the field to rest: and let's away,
To part the glories of this happy day.

      [*Exeunt.*

GLOSSARY

References are given only for words having more than one meaning, the first use of each sense being then noted.

Abate, *v.t.* to diminish. M.N.D. III. 2. 432. Deduct, except. L.L.L. v. 2. 539. Cast down. Cor. III. 3. 134. Blunt. R III. v. 5. 35. Deprive. Lear, II. 4. 159.

Abatement, *sb.* diminution Lear, I. 4. 59. Depreciation. Tw.N. I. 1. 13.

Abjects, *sb.* outcasts, servile persons.

Able, *v.t.* to warrant.

Abode, *v.t.* to forebode. 3 H VI. v. 6. 45.

Abode, *sb.* stay, delay. M. of V. II. 6. 77.

Abodements, *sb.* forebodings.

Abram, *adj.* auburn.

Abridgement, *sb.* short entertainment, for pastime.

Abrook, *v.t.* to brook, endure.

Absey book, *sb.* ABC book, or primer.

Absolute, *adj.* resolved. M. for M. III. 1. 5. Positive. Cor. III. 2. 39. Perfect. H V. III. 7. 26. Complete. Tp. I. 2. 109; Lucr. 853.

Aby, *v.t.* to atone for, expiate.

Accite, *v.t.* to cite, summon.

Acknown, *adj.* cognisant.

Acture, *sb.* performance.

Addition, *sb.* title, attribute.

Adoptious, *adj.* given by adoption.

Advice, *sb.* consideration.

Aery, *sb.* eagle's nest or brood. R III. I. 3. 265, 271. Hence generally any brood. Ham. II. 2. 344.

Affectioned, *p.p.* affected.

Affeered, *p.p.* sanctioned, confirmed.

Affiance, *sb.* confidence, trust.

Affined, *p.p.* related. T. & C. I. 3. 25. Bound. Oth. I. 1. 39.

Affront, *v.t.* to confront, meet.

Affy, *v.t.* to betroth. 2 H VI. IV . 1. 80. *v.t.* to trust. T.A. I.1. 47.

Aglet-baby, *sb.* small figure cut on the tag of a lace (Fr. *aiguillette*). T. of S. I. 2. 78.

Agnize, *v.t.* to acknowledge, confess.

Agood, *adv.* much.

Aim, *sb.* a guess.

Aim, to cry aim, to encourage, an archery term.

Alderliefest, *adj.* most loved of all.

Ale, *sb.* alehouse.

All amort, completely dejected (Fr. *a la mort*).

Allicholy, *sb.* melancholy.

Allow, *v.t.* to approve.

Allowance, *sb.* acknowledgement, approval.

Ames-ace, *sb.* the lowest throw of the dice.

Anchor, *sb.* anchorite, hermit.

Ancient, *sb.* ensign, standard. 1 H IV. IV. 2. 32. Ensign, ensign-bearer. 1 H IV. IV. 2. 24.

Ancientry, *sb.* antiquity, used of old people, W.T. III. 3. 62. Of the gravity which belongs to antiquity, M.A. II. 1. 75.

Angel, *sb.* gold coin, worth about 10s.

Antic, *adj.* fantastic. Ham. I. 5. 172.

Antick, *v.t.* to make a buffoon of. A. & C. II. 7. 126.

Antick, *sb.* buffoon of the old plays.

Appeal, *sb.* impeachment.

Appeal, *v.t.* to impeach.

Apperil, *sb.* peril.

Apple-john, *sb.* a shrivelled winter apple.

Argal, corruption of the Latin *ergo*, therefore.

Argo, corruption of *ergo*, therefore.

Aroint thee, begone, get thee gone.

Articulate, *v.i.* to make articles of peace. Cor. I. 9. 75. *v.t.* to set forth in detail. 1 H IV. V. 1. 72.

Artificial, *adj.* working by art.

Askance, *v.t.* to make look askance or sideways, make to avert.

Aspic, *sb.* asp.

Assured, *p.p.* betrothed.

Atone, *v.t.* to reconcile. R II. I. 1. 202. Agree. As V. 4. 112.

Attorney, *sb.* proxy, agent.

Attorneyed, *p.p.* done by proxy. W T. I. I. 28. Engaged as
an attorney, M. for M. V. I. 383.

Attribute, *sb.* reputation.

Avail, *sb.* profit.

Avise, *v.t.* to inform. Are you avised? = Do you know?

Awful, *adj.* filled with regard for authority.

Awkward, *adj.* contrary.

Baby, *sb.* a doll.

Baccare, go back, a spurious Latin word.

Back-trick, a caper backwards in dancing.

Baffle, *v.t.* to disgrace (a recreant knight).

Bale, *sb.* evil, mischief.

Ballow, *sb.* cudgel.

Ban, *v.t.* curse. 2 H VI. II. 4. 25. *sb.* a curse. Ham. III. 2. 269.

Band, *sb.* bond.

Bank, *v.t.* sail along the banks of.

Bare, *v.t.* to shave.

Barn, *v.t.* to put in a barn.

Barn, or Barne, *sb.* bairn, child.

Base, *sb.* a rustic game. Bid the base = Challenge to a race.
Two G. I. 2. 97.

Bases, *sb.* knee-length skirts worn by mounted knights.

Basilisco-like, Basilisco, a character in the play of *Soliman
and Perseda*.

Basilisk, *sb.* a fabulous serpent. H V. V. 2. 17. A large
cannon. 1 H IV. II. 3. 57.

Bate, *sb.* strife.

Bate, *v.i.* flutter as a hawk. 1 H IV. IV. 1. 99. Diminish. 1 H
IV. III. 3. 2.

Bate, *v.t.* abate. Tp. I. 2. 250. Beat down, weaken. M. of V.
III. 3. 32.

Bavin, *adj.* made of bavin or brushwood. 1 H IV. III. 2. 61.

Bawbling, *adj.* trifling, insignificant.

Baw-cock, *sb.* fine fellow (Fr. *beau coq.*) H V. III. 2. 25.

Bay, *sb.* space between the main timbers in a roof.

Beadsman, *sb.* one who is hired to offer prayers for another.

Bearing-cloth, *sb.* the cloth in which a child was carried to be christened.

Bear in hand, to deceive with false hopes.

Beat, *v.i.* to meditate. 2 H IV. II. 1. 20. Throb. Lear, III. 4. 14.

Becoming, *sb.* grace.

Beetle, *sb.* a heavy mallet, 2 H IV. I. 2. 235. Beetle-headed = heavy, stupid. T. of S. IV. 1. 150.

Behave, *v.t.* to control.

Behest, *sb.* command.

Behove, *sb.* behoof.

Be-lee'd, *p.p.* forced to lee of the wind.

Bench, *v.i.* to seat on the bench of justice. Lear, III. 6. 38. *v.t.* to elevate to the bench. W.T. I .2. 313.

Bench-hole, the hole of a privy.

Bergomask, a rustic dance, named from Bergamo in Italy.

Beshrew, *v.t.* to curse; but not used seriously.

Besort, *v.t.* to fit, suit.

Bestraught, *adj.* distraught.

Beteem, *v.t.* to permit, grant.

Bezonian, *sb.* a base and needy fellow.

Bias, *adj.* curving like the bias side of a bowling bowl.

Biggen, *sb.* a nightcap.

Bilbo, *sb.* a Spanish rapier, named from Bilbao or Bilboa.

Bilboes, *sb.* stocks used for punishment on shipboard.

Birdbolt, *sb.* a blunt-headed arrow used for birds.

Bisson, *adj.* dim-sighted. Cor. II. 1. 65. Bisson rheum = blinding tears. Ham. II. 2. 514.

Blacks, *sb.* black mourning clothes.

Blank, *sb.* the white mark in the centre of a target.

Blank, *v.t.* to blanch, make pale.

Blanks, *sb.* royal charters left blank to be filled in as occasion dictated.

Blench, *sb.* a swerve, inconsistency.

Blistered, *adj.* padded out, puffed.

Block, *sb.* the wood on which hats are made. M.A. I. 1. 71. Hence, the style of hat. Lear, IV. 6. 185.

Blood-boltered, *adj.* clotted with blood.

Blowse, *sb.* a coarse beauty.

Bob, *sb.* smart rap, jest.

Bob, *v.t.* to beat hard, thwack. R III. V. 3. 335. To obtain by fraud, cheat. T. & C. III. 1. 69.

Bodge, *v.i.* to budge.

Bodkin, *sb.* small dagger, stiletto.

Boggle, *v.i.* to swerve, shy, hesitate.

Boggler, *sb.* swerver.

Boln, *adj.* swollen.

Bolt, *v.t.* to sift, refine.

Bolter, *sb.* a sieve.

Bombard, *sb.* a leathern vessel for liquor.

Bona-robas, *sb.* flashily dressed women of easy virtue.

Bonnet, *v.i.* to doff the hat, be courteous.

Boot, *sb.* profit. 1 H VI. IV. 6. 52. That which is given over and above. R III. IV. 4. 65. Booty. 3 H VI. IV. 1. 13.

Boots, *sb.* Give me not the boots = do not inflict on me the torture of the boots, which were employed to wring confessions.

Bosky, *adj.* woody.

Botcher, *sb.* patcher of old clothes.

Bots, *sb.* small worms in horses.

Bottled, *adj.* big-bellied.

Brabble, *sb.* quarrel, brawl.

Brabbler, *sb.* a brawler.

Brach, *sb.* a hound-bitch.

Braid, *adj.* deceitful.

Braid, *v.t.* to upbraid, reproach.

Brain, *v.t.* to conceive in the brain.

Brazed, *p.p.* made like brass, perhaps hardened in the fire.

Breeched, *p.p.* as though wearing breeches. Mac. II. 3. 120.

Breeching, *adj.* liable to be breeched for a flogging.

Breese, *sb.* a gadfly.

Brib'd-buck, *sb.* perhaps a buck distributed in presents.

Brock, *sb.* badger.

Broken, *adj.* of a mouth with some teeth missing.

Broker, *sb*. agent, go-between.

Brownist, a follower of Robert Brown, the founder of the sect of Independents.

Buck, *v.t*. to wash and beat linen.

Buck-basket, *sb*. a basket to take linen to be bucked.

Bucking, *sb*. washing.

Buckle, *v.i*. to encounter hand to hand, cope. 1. H VI. I. 2. 95. To bow. 2 H VI. I. 1. 141.

Budget, *sb*. a leather scrip or bag.

Bug, *sb*. bugbear, a thing causing terror.

Bugle, *sb*. a black bead.

Bully, *sb*. a fine fellow.

Bully-rook, *sb*. a swaggering cheater.

Bung, *sb*. pickpocket.

Burgonet, *sb*. close-fitting Burgundian helmet.

Busky, *adj*. woody.

By-drinkings, *sb*. drinks taken between meals.

Caddis, *sb*. worsted trimming, galloon.

Cade, *sb*. cask, barrel.

Caitiff, *sb*. captive, slave, a wretch. *adj*. R II. I. 2. 53.

Caliver, *sb*. musket.

Callet, *sb*. trull, drab.

Calling, *sb*. appellation.

Calm, *sb*. qualm.

Canaries = quandary.

Canary, *sb*. a lively Spanish dance. *v.i*. to dance canary.

Canker, *sb*. the dog-rose or wild-rose. 1 H IV. I. 3. 176. A worm that destroys blossoms. M.N.D. II. 2.3.

Canstick, *sb*. candlestick.

Cantle, *sb*. piece, slice.

Canton, *sb*. canto.

Canvass, *v.t*. shake as in a sieve, take to task.

Capable, *adj*. sensible. As III. 5. 23. Sensitive, susceptible. Ham. III. 4. 128. Comprehensive. Oth. III. 3. 459. Able to possess. Lear, II. 1. 85.

Capocchia, *sb*. the feminine of capocchio (Ital.), simpleton.

Capriccio, *sb.* caprice, fancy.

Captious, *adj.* either a contraction of capacious or a coined word meaning capable of receiving.

Carack, *sb.* a large merchant ship.

Carbonado, *sb.* meat scotched for boiling. *v.t.* to hack like a carbonado.

Card, *sb.* a cooling card = a sudden and decisive stroke.

Card, *v.t.* to mix (liquids).

Cardecu, *sb.* quarter of a French crown (*quart d'écu*).

Care, *v.i.* to take care.

Careire, career, *sb.* a short gallop at full speed.

Carlot, *sb.* peasant.

Carpet consideration, On, used of those made knights for court services, not for valour in the field.

Carpet-mongers, *sb.* carpet-knights.

Carpets, *sb.* tablecloths.

Case, *v.t.* to strip off the case or skin of an animal. A.W. III. 6. 103. Put on a mask. 1 H IV. II. 2. 55.

Case, *sb.* skin of an animal. Tw.N. V. 1.163. A set, as of musical instruments, which were in fours. H V. III. 2. 4.

Cashiered, *p.p.* discarded; in M.W.W. I. 1. 168 it probably means relieved of his cash.

Cataian, *sb.* a native of Cathay, a Chinaman; a cant word.

Cater-cousins, good friends.

Catlings, *sb.* catgut strings for musical instruments.

Cautel, *sb.* craft, deceit, stratagem.

Cautelous, *adj.* crafty, deceitful.

Ceased, *p.p.* put off.

Censure, *sb.* opinion, judgement.

Certify, *v.t.* to inform, make certain.

Cess, *sb.* reckoning; out of all cess = immoderately.

Cesse = cease.

Champain, *sb.* open country.

Channel, *sb.* gutter.

Chape, *sb.* metal end of a scabbard.

Chapless, *adj.* without jaws.

Charact, *sb.* a special mark or sign of office.

Chare, *sb.* a turn of work.

Charge, *sb.* weight, importance. W.T. IV. 3. 258. Cost, expense. John I. 1. 49.

Chaudron, *sb.* entrails.

Check, *sb.* rebuke, reproof.

Check, *v.t.* to rebuke, chide.

Check, *v.i.* to start on sighting game.

Cherry-pit, *sb.* a childish game consisting of pitching cherry-stones into a small hole.

Cheveril, *sb.* leather of kid skin. R. & J. II. 3. 85. *adj.* Tw.N. III. 1. 12.

Che vor ye = I warn you.

Chewet, *sb.* chough. 1 H IV. V. 1. 29. (Fr. *chouette* or *chutte*). Perhaps with play on other meaning of chewet, *i.e.*, a kind of meat pie.

Childing, *adj.* fruitful.

Chop, *v.t.* to clop, pop.

Chopine, *sb.* shoe with a high sole.

Choppy, *adj.* chapped.

Christendom, *sb.* Christian name.

Chuck, *sb.* chick, term of endearment.

Chuff, *sb.* churl, boor.

Cinque pace, *sb.* a slow stately dance. M.A. II. 1. 72. Compare sink-a-pace in Tw.N. I. 3. 126.

Cipher, *v.t.* to decipher.

Circumstance, *sb.* particulars, details. Two G. I. 1. 36. Ceremonious phrases. M. of V. I. 1. 154.

Circumstanced, *p.p.* swayed by circumstance.

Citizen, *adj.* town-bred, effeminate.

Cittern, *sb.* guitar.

Clack-dish, *sb.* wooden dish carried by beggars.

Clamour, *v.t.* to silence.

Clapper-claw, *v.t.* to thrash, drub.

Claw, *v.t.* to scratch, flatter.

Clepe, *v.t.* to call.

Cliff, *sb.* clef, the key in music.

Cling, *v.t.* to make shrivel up.

Clinquant, *adj.* glittering with gold or silver lace or decorations.

Close, *sb.* cadence in music. R II. II. 1. 12. *adj.* secret. T. of S. Ind. I. 127. *v.i.* to come to an agreement, make terms. Two G. II. 5. 12.

Closely, *adv.* secretly.

Clout, *sb.* bull's-eye of a target.

Clouted, *adj.* hobnailed (others explain as patched).

Cobloaf, *sb.* a crusty, ill-shapen loaf.

Cockered, *p.p.* pampered.

Cockle, *sb.* the corncockle weed.

Cockney, *sb.* a city-bred person, a foolish wanton.

Cock-shut time, *sb.* twilight.

Codding, *adj.* lascivious.

Codling, *sb.* an unripe apple.

Cog, *v.i.* to cheat. R III I. 3. 48. *v.t.* to get by cheating, filch. Cor. III. 2. 133.

Coistrel, *sb.* groom.

Collection, *sb.* inference.

Collied, *p.p.* blackened, darkened.

Colour, *sb.* pretext. Show no colour, or bear no colour = allow of no excuse.

Colours, fear no colours = fear no enemy, be afraid of nothing.

Colt, *v.t.* to make a fool of, gull.

Combinate, *adj.* betrothed.

Combine, *v.t.* to bind.

Comfect, *sb.* comfit.

Commodity, *sb.* interest, advantage. John, II. 1. 573. Cargo of merchandise. Tw.N. III. 1. 46.

Comparative, *adj.* fertile in comparisons. 1 H IV. I. 2. 83.

Comparative, *sb.* a rival in wit. 1 H IV. III. 2. 67.

Compassed, *adj.* arched, round.

Complexion, *sb.* temperament.

Comply, *v.i.* to be ceremonious.

Composition, *sb.* agreement, consistency.

Composture, *sb.* compost.

Composure, *sb.* composition. T. & C. II. 3. 238; A. & C. I. 4. 22. Compact. T. & C. II. 3. 100.

Compt. *sb.* account, reckoning.

Comptible, *adj.* susceptible, sensitive.

Con, *v.t.* to study, learn; con thanks = give thanks.

Conceptious, *adj.* apt at conceiving.

Conclusion, *sb.* experiment.

Condolement, *sb.* lamentation. Ham. I. 2. 93. Consolation, Per. II. 1. 150.

Conduce, *v.i.* perhaps to tend to happen.

Conduct, *sb.* guide, escort.

Confiners, *sb.* border peoples.

Confound, *v.t.* to waste. 1 H IV. I. 3. 100. Destroy. M. of V. III. 2. 278.

Congied, *p.p.* taken leave (Fr. *congé*).

Consent, *sb.* agreement, plot.

Consist, *v.i.* to insist.

Consort, *sb.* company, fellowship. Two G. III. 2. 84; IV. 1. 64. *v.t.* to accompany. C. of E. I. 2. 28.

Conspectuity, *sb.* power of vision.

Constant, *adj.* consistent.

Constantly, *adv.* firmly, surely.

Conster, *v.t.* to construe, interpret.

Constringed, *p.p.* compressed.

Consul, *sb.* senator.

Containing, *sb.* contents.

Contraction, *sb.* the making of the marriage-contract.

Contrive, *v.t.* to wear out, spend. T. of S. I. 2. 273. Conspire. J.C. II. 3. 16.

Control, *v.t.* to check, contradict.

Convent, *v.t.* to summon.

Convert, *v.i.* to change.

Convertite, *sb.* a penitent.

Convince, *v.t.* to overcome. Mac. I. 7. 64. Convict. T. & C. II. 2. 130.

Convive, *v.i.* to banquet together.

Convoy, *sb.* conveyance, escort.

Copatain hat, *sb.* a high-crowned hat.

Cope, *v.t.* to requite. M. of V. IV. 1. 412.

Copesmate, *sb.* a companion.

Copped, *adj.* round-topped.

Copulatives, *sb.* persons desiring to be coupled in marriage.

Copy, *sb.* theme, text. C. of E. V. 1. 62. Tenure. Mac. III. 2. 37.

Coranto, *sb.* a quick, lively dance.

Corky, *adj.* shrivelled (with age).

Cornet, *sb.* a band of cavalry.

Corollary, *sb.* a supernumerary.

Cosier, *sb.* botcher, cobbler.

Costard, *sb.* an apple, the head (slang).

Cote, *v.t.* to come up with, pass on the way.

Cot-quean, *sb.* a man who busies himself in women's affairs.

Couch, *v.t.* to make to cower.

Counter, *adv.* to run or hunt counter is to trace the scent of the game backwards.

Counter, *sb.* a metal disk used in reckoning.

Counter-caster, *sb.* one who reckons by casting up counters.

Countermand, *v.t.* to prohibit, keep in check. C. of E. IV. 2. 37. Contradict. Lucr. 276.

Countervail, *v.t.* to outweigh.

County, *sb.* count. As II. 1. 67.

Couplet, *sb.* a pair.

Courser's hair, a horse's hair laid in water was believed to turn into a serpent.

Court holy-water, *sb.* flattery.

Courtship, *sb.* courtly manners.

Convent, *sb.* a convent.

Cox my passion = God's passion.

Coy, *v.t.* to fondle, caress. M.N.D. IV. 1. 2. *v.i.* to disdain. Cor. V. 1. 6.

Crack, *v.i.* to boast. *sb.* an urchin.

Crank, *sb.* winding passage. *v.i.* to wind, twist.

Crants, *sb.* garland, chaplet.

Crare, *sb.* a small sailing vessel.

Crisp, *adj.* curled.

Cross, *sb.* a coin (stamped with a cross).

Cross-row, *sb.* alphabet.

Crow-keeper, *sb.* a boy, or scare-crow, to keep crows from corn.

Cullion, *sb.* a base fellow.

Cunning, *sb.* knowledge, skill. *adj.* knowing, skilful, skilfully wrought.

Curb, *v.i.* to bow, cringe obsequiously.

Curdied, *p.p.* congealed.

Curiosity, *sb.* scrupulous nicety.

Curst, *adj.* bad-tempered.

Curtal, *adj.* having a docked tail. *sb.* a dock-tailed horse.

Customer, *sb.* a loose woman.

Cut, *sb.* a bobtailed horse.

Cuttle, *sb.* a bully.

Daff, *v.t.* to doff. Daff aside = thrust aside slightingly.

Darraign, *v.t.* to arrange, order the ranks for battle.

Dash, *sb.* mark of disgrace.

Daubery, *sb.* false pretence, cheat.

Day-woman, *sb.* dairy-woman.

Debosht, *p.p.* debauched.

Deck, *sb.* pack of cards.

Deem, *sb.* doom; opinion.

Defeat, *v.t.* to disguise. Oth. I. 3. 333. Destroy. Oth. IV. 2. 160.

Defeature, *sb.* disfigurement.

Defend, *v.t.* to forbid.

Defuse, *v.t.* to disorder and make unrecognizable.

Defused, *p.p.* disordered, shapeless.

Demerit, *sb.* desert.

Denier, *sb.* a small French coin.

Dern, *adj.* secret, dismal.

Detect, *v.t.* to discover, disclose.

Determinate, *p.p.* determined upon. Tw.N. II. 1. 10. Decided. Oth. IV. 2. 229. Ended. Sonn. LXXXVII. 4. *v.t.* bring to an end. R II. 1. 3.

Dich, *v.i.* do to, happen to.

Diet, *v.t.* keep strictly, as if by a prescribed regimen.

Diffidence, *sb.* distrust, suspicion.

Digression, *sb.* transgression.

Diminutives, *sb.* the smallest of coins.

Directitude, *sb.* a blunder for some word unknown. Cor. IV. 5. 205.

Disanimate, *v.t.* to discourage.

Disappointed, *p.p.* unprepared.

Discandy, *v.i.* to thaw, melt.

Discipled, *p.p.* taught.

Disclose, *v.t.* to hatch. *sb.* the breaking of the shell by the chick on hatching.

Disme, *sb.* a tenth.

Distain, *v.t.* to stain, pollute.

Dive-dapper, *sb.* dabchick.

Dividant, *adj.* separate, different.

Dotant, *sb.* dotard.

Doubt, *sb.* fear, apprehension.

Dout, *v.t.* to extinguish.

Dowlas, *sb.* coarse linen.

Dowle, *sb.* down, the soft plumage of a feather.

Down-gyved, *adj.* hanging down about the ankle like gyves.

Dribbling, *adj.* weakly shot.

Drugs, *sb.* drudges.

Drumble, *v.i.* to be sluggish or clumsy.

Dry-beat, *v.t.* to cudgel, thrash.

Dry-foot. To draw dry-foot, track by scent.

Dudgeon, *sb.* the handle of a dagger.

Due, *v.t.* to endue.

Dump, *sb.* a sad strain.

Dup, *v.t.* to open.

Ean, *v.i.* to yean, lamb.

Ear, *v.t.* to plough, till.

Eche, *v.t.* to eke out.

Eftest, *adv.* readiest.

Eftsoons, *adv.* immediately.

Egal, *adj.* equal.

Egally, *adv.* equally.

Eisel, *sb.* vinegar.

Elf, *v.t.* to mat hair in a tangle; believed to be the work of elves.

Emballing, *sb.* investiture with the crown and sceptre.

Embarquement, *sb.* hindrance, restraint.

Ember-eyes, *sb.* vigils of Ember days.

Embowelled, *p.p.* emptied, exhausted.

Emmew, *v.t.* perhaps to mew up.

Empiricutic, *adj.* empirical, quackish.

Emulation, *sb.* jealous rivalry.

Enacture, *sb.* enactment, performance.

Encave, *v.t.* to hide, conceal.

Encumbered, *p.p.* folded.

End, *sb.* still an end = continually.

End, *v.t.* to get in the harvest.

Englut, *v.t.* to swallow.

Enlargement, *sb.* liberty, liberation.

Enormous, *adj.* out of the norm, monstrous.

Enseamed, *p.p.* defiled, filthy.

Ensear, *v.t.* to sear up, make dry.

Enshield, *adj.* enshielded, protected.

Entertain, *v.t.* to take into one's service.

Entertainment, *sb.* service.

Entreat, *v.t.* to treat.

Entreatments, *sb.* invitations.

Ephesian, *sb.* boon companion.

Eryngoes, *sb.* roots of the sea-holly, a supposed aphrodisiac.

Escot, *v.t.* to pay for.

Espial, *sb.* a spy.

Even Christian, *sb.* fellow Christian.

Excrement, *sb.* anything that grows out of the body, as hair, nails, etc. Used of the beard. M. of V. III. 2. 84. Of the hair. C. of E. II. 2. 79. Of the moustache. L.L.L. V. 1. 98.

Exhibition, *sb.* allowance, pension.

Exigent, *sb.* end. 1 H VI. II. 5. 9. Exigency, critical need. J. C. V. 1. 19.

Exion, *sb.* blunder for action.

Expiate, *v.t* . to terminate. Sonn. XXII. 4.

Expiate, *p.p.* ended. R III. III. 3. 24.

Exsufflicate, *adj.* inflated, both literally and metaphorically.

Extent, *sb.* seizure. As III. 1. 17. Violent attack. Tw.N. IV. 1. 51. Condescension, favour. Ham. II. 2. 377. Display. T. A. IV. 4. 3.

Extraught, *p.p.* extracted.

Extravagancy, *sb.* vagrancy, aimless wandering about.

Eyas, *sb.* a nestling, a young hawk just taken from the nest.

Eyas-musket, *sb.* the young sparrow-hawk.

Eye, *v.i.* to appear, look to the eye.

Facinerious, *adj.* wicked.

Fadge, *v.i.* to succeed, suit.

Fading, *sb.* the burden of a song.

Fair, *v.t.* to make beautiful.

Fairing, *sb.* a gift.

Faitor, *sb.* evil-doer.

Fangled, *adj.* fond of novelties.

Fap, *adj.* drunk.

Farced, *p.p.* stuffed out.

Fardel, *sb.* a burden, bundle.

Fat, *adj.* cloying. *sb.* vat.

Favour, *sb.* outward appearance, aspect. In pl. = features.

Fear, *v.t.* to frighten. 3 H VI. III. 3. 226. Fear for. M. of V. III. 5. 3.

Feat, *adj.* neat, dexterous.

Feat, *v.t.* to fashion, form.

Fee, *sb.* worth, value.

Feeder, *sb.* servant.

Fee-farm, *sb.* a tenure without limit of time.

Fellowly, *adj.* companionable, sympathetic.

Feodary, *sb.* confederate.

Fere, *sb.* spouse, consort.

Ferret, *v.t.* to worry.

Festinate, *adj.* swift, speedy.

Fet, *p.p.* fetched.

Fico, *sb.* a fig (Span.).

File, *sb.* list.

File, *v.t.* to defile. Mac. III. 1. 65. Smooth, polish. L.L.L. V. I. II. *v.i.* to walk in file. H VIII. III. 2. 171.

Fill-horse, *sb.* a shaft-horse.

Fills, *sb.* shafts.

Fineless, *adj.* endless, infinite.

Firago, *sb.* virago.

Firk, *v.t.* to beat.

Fitchew, *sb.* pole-cat.

Fitment, *sb.* that which befits.

Flap-dragon, *sb.* snap-dragon, or small burning object, lighted and floated in a glass of liquor, to be swallowed burning. L.L.L. V. I. 43. 2 H IV. II. 4. 244. *v.t.* to swallow like a flap-dragon. W.T. III. 3.100.

Flaw, *sb.* gust of wind. Ham. V. 1. 223. Small flake of ice. 2 H IV. IV. 4. 35. Passionate outburst. M. for M. II. 3. 11. A crack. Lear, II. 4. 288. *v.t.* make a flaw in, break. H VIII. I. 1. 95; I. 2. 21.

Fleer, *sb.* sneer. Oth. IV. 1. 83. *v.i.* to grin; sneer. L.L.L. V. 2. 109.

Fleshment, *sb.* encouragement given by first success.

Flewed, *p.p.* with large hanging chaps.

Flight, *sb.* a long light arrow.

Flighty, *adj.* swift.

Flirt-gill, *sb.* light wench.

Flote, *sb.* sea.

Flourish, *v.t.* to ornament, gloss over.

Fobbed, *p.p.* cheated, deceived.

Foil, *sb.* defeat. 1 H VI. III. 3. 11. *v.t.* to defeat, mar. Pass. P. 99

Foin, *v.i.* to thrust (in fencing).

Fopped, *p.p.* cheated, fooled.

Forbod, *p.p.* forbidden.

Fordo, *v.t.* to undo, destroy.

Foreign, *adj.* dwelling abroad.

Fork, *sb.* the forked tongue of a snake. M. for M. III. 1. 16. The barbed head of an arrow. Lear, I. 1. 146. The junction of the legs with the trunk. Lear. IV. 6. 120.

Forked, *p.p.* barbed. As II. 1. 24. Horned as a cuckold. T. & C. I. 2. 164.

Forslow, *v.i.* to delay.

Forspeak, *v.t.* to speak against.

Fosset-seller, *sb.* a seller of taps.

Fox, *sb.* broadsword.

Foxship, *sb.* selfish and ungrateful, cunning.

Fracted, *p.p.* broken.

Frampold, *adj.* turbulent, quarrelsome.

Frank, *v.t.* to pen in a frank or sty. R III. 1. 3. 314. *sb.* a sty. 2 H IV. II. 2. 145. *adj.* liberal. Lear, III. 4. 20.

Franklin, *sb.* a yeoman.

Fraught, *sb.* freight, cargo, load. Tw.N. V. 1. 59. *v.t.* to load, burden. Cym. I. 1. 126. *p.p.* laden. M. of V. II. 8. 30. Stored. Two G. III. 2. 70.

Fraughtage, *sb.* cargo. C. of E. IV. 1. 8.

Fraughting, *part. adj.* constituting the cargo.

Frize, *sb.* a kind of coarse woollen cloth with a nap.

Frontier, *sb.* an outwork in fortification. 1 H IV. II. 3. 56. Used figuratively. 1 H IV. I. 3. 19.

Fruitful, *adj.* bountiful, plentiful.

Frush, *v.t.* to bruise, batter.

Frutify, blunder for certify. M. of V II. 2. 132.

Fubbed off, *p.p.* put off with excuses. 2 H IV. II. 1. 34.

Fullams, *sb.* a kind of false dice.

Gad, *sb.* a pointed instrument. T.A. IV. 1. 104. Upon the gad = on the spur of the moment, hastily. Lear, I. 2. 26.

Gage, *v.t.* to pledge.

Gaingiving, *sb.* misgiving.

Galliard, *sb.* a lively dance.

Gallimaufry, *sb.* medley, tumble.

Gallow, *v.t.* to frighten.

Gallowglass, *sb.* heavy- armed Irish foot-soldier.

Gallows, *sb.* a rogue, one fit to be hung.

Gallows-bird, *sb.* one that merits hanging.

Garboil, *sb.* uproar, commotion.

Gaskins, *sb.* loose breeches.

Gastness, *sb.* ghastliness, terror.

Geck, *sb.* dupe.

Generation, *sb.* offspring.

Generous, *adj.* nobly born.

Gennet, *sb.* a Spanish horse.

Gentry, *sb.* rank by birth. M.W. W. II. 1. 51. Courtesy. Ham. II. 2. 22.

German, *sb.* a near kinsman.

Germen, *sb.* germ, seed.

Gest, *sb.* a period of sojourn; originally the halting place in a royal progress.

Gib, *sb.* an old rom-cat.

Gibbet, *v.t.* to hang, as a barrel when it is slung.

Gig, *sb.* top.

Giglot, *adj.* wanton. 1 H VI. IV. 7. 41. *sb.* M. for M. V. 1. 345.

Gillyvors, *sb.* gillyflowers.

Gimmal-bit, *sb.* a double bit, or one made with double rings.

Gimmer, *sb.* contrivance, mechanical device.

Ging, *sb.* gang, pack.

Gird, *sb.* a scoff, jest. 2 H VI. III. 1. 131. *v.t.* to taunt, gibe at. 2 H IV. I. 2. 6.

Gleek, *sb.* scoff. 1 H VI. IV. 2. 12. *v.i.* to scoff. M.N.D. III. 1. 145.

Glib, *v.t.* to geld.

Gloze, *v.i.* to comment. H V. I. 2. 40. T. & C. II. 2. 165. To use flattery. R II. II. 1. 10; T.A. IV. 4. 35.

Gnarling, *pr.p.* snarling.

Godden, *sb.* good den, good even.

God'ild, God yield, God reward.

God-jer = good-year.

Good-year, *sb.* a meaningless interjection. M.A. I. 3. 1.
Some malific power. Lear, V. 3. 24.

Goss, *sb.* gorse.

Gossip, *sb.* sponsor. Two G. III. 1. 269. *v.t.* to stand
sponsor for. A. W. I. 1. 176.

Gorbellied, *adj.* big-bellied.

Graff, *sb.* graft, scion. *v.t.* to graft.

Grain, *sb.* a fast colour. Hence in grain = ingrained.

Gratillity, *sb.* gratuity.

Gratulate, *adj.* gratifying.

Greek, *sb.* boon companion.

Grise, *sb.* a step.

Guard, *v.t.* to trim, ornament.

Guardant, *sb.* sentinel, guard.

Guidon, *sb.* standard, banner.

Gules, *adj.* red, in heraldry.

Gust, *sb.* taste. *v.t.* to taste.

Hackney, *sb.* loose woman.

Haggard, *sb.* untrained hawk.

Haggled, *p.p.* hacked, mangled.

Hair, *sb.* texture, nature. 1 H IV. IV. 1. 61. Against the hair
= against the grain. R. & J. II. 3. 97.

Handfast, *sb.* betrothal, contract. Cym. I. 5. 78. Custody.
W.T. IV. 3. 778.

Handsaw, *sb.* corruption of heronshaw, a heron.

Hardiment, *sb.* daring deed.

Harlot, *adj.* lewd, base.

Hatched, *p.p.* closed with a hatch or half door. Per. IV. 2.
33. Engraved. T. & C. I. 3. 65.

Havoc, to cry havoc = cry no quarter. John, II. 1. 357. *v.t.*
cut to pieces, destroy. H V. I. 2. 193.

Hawking, *adj.* hawk-like.

Hay, *sb.* a round dance. L.L.L. V. 1. 147. A term in fencing when a hit is made (Ital. *hai*, you have it). R. & J. II. 4. 27.

Hebenon, *sb.* perhaps the yew (Germ. *Eiben*). Ebony and henbane have been suggested.

Hefts, *sb.* heavings.

Helm, *v.t.* to steer.

Helpless, *adj.* not helping, useless. R III. 1. 2. 13; Lucr. 1027. Incurable, Lucr. 756.

Hent, *sb.* grasp, hold. Ham. III. 3. 88. *v.t.* to hold, pass. M. for M. IV. 6. 14.

Hermit, *sb.* beadsman, one bound to pray for another.

Hild = held.

Hilding, *sb.* a good-for-nothing.

Hoar, *adj.* mouldy, R. & J. II. 3. 136. *v.i.* to become mouldy. R. & J. II. 3. 142.

Hoar, *v.t.* to make hoary or white, as with leprosy.

Hobby-horse, *sb.* a principal figure in the old morris dance. L.L.L. III. 1. 30. A light woman. M.A. III. 2. 68.

Hob-nob, have or not have, hit or miss.

Hold in, *v.i.* to keep counsel.

Holding, *sb.* the burden of a song. A. & C. II. 7. 112. Fitness, sense. A.W. IV. 2. 27.

Holy-ales, *sb.* rural festivals.

Honest, *adj.* chaste.

Honesty, *sb.* chastity. M.W.W. II. 2. 234. Decency. Tw.N. II. 3. 85. Generosity, liberality. Tim. III. 1. 30.

Honey-seed, blunder for homicide, 2 H IV. II. 1. 52.

Honey-suckle, blunder for homicidal. 2 H IV. II. 1. 50.

Hoodman, *sb.* the person blinded in the game of hoodman-blind.

Hoodman-blind, *sb.* blind-man's buff.

Hot at hand, not to be held in.

Hot-house, *sb.* bagnio, often in fact a brothel as well.

Hox, *v.t.* to hough, hamstring.

Hoy, *sb.* a small coasting vessel.

Hugger-mugger, In, stealthily and secretly.

Hull, *v.i.* to float.

Hulling, *pr. p.* floating at the mercy of the waves.

Ignomy, *sb.* ignominy.

Imbar, *v.t.* to bar in, make secure. H V. I. 2. 94.

Imboss, *v.t.* to hunt to death.

Imbossed, *p.p.* swollen. As II. 7. 67. Foaming at the mouth. T. of S. Ind. I. 16.

Immanity, *sb.* savageness, ferocity.

Immoment, *adj.* insignificant.

Immures, *sb.* surrounding walls.

Imp, *v.t.* to graft new feathers to a falcon's wing.

Impair, *adj.* unsuitable.

Impale, *v.t.* to encircle.

Impart, *v.t.* to afford, grant. Lucr. 1039; Sonn. LXXII. 8. *v.i.* to behave oneself. Ham. I. 2. 112.

Imperceiverant, *adj.* lacking in perception.

Impeticos, *v.t.* to put in the petticoat or pocket.

Importance, *sb.* importunity. John, II. 1. 7. Import. W.T. V. 2. 19. Question at issue, that which is imported. Cym. I. 5. 40.

Imposition, *sb.* command, injunction. M. of V. I. 2. 106. Penalty. M. for M. I. 2. 186.

Imposthume, *sb.* abscess.

Imprese, *sb.* device with a motto.

Include, *v.t.* to conclude, end.

Incontinent, *adj.* immediate.

Incony, *adj.* dainty, delicate.

Indent, *v.i.* to make terms.

Index, *sb.* introduction (in old books the index came first).

Indifferency, *sb.* impartiality.

Indirectly, *adv.* wrongly, unjustly.

Indurance, *sb.* durance, imprisonment.

Infest, *v.t.* to vex, trouble.

Inherit, *v.t.* to possess. Tp. IV. 1. 154. To cause to possess, put in possession. R II. I. 1. 85. *v.i.* to take possession. Tp. II. 2. 182.

Inheritor, *sb.* possessor.

Injury, *sb*. insult.

Inkhorn mate, *sb*. bookworm.

Inkle, *sb*. coarse tape.

Insisture, *sb*. persistence.

Intenible, *adj*. incapable of holding.

Intention, *sb*. aim, direction.

Intermissive, *adj*. intermitted, interrupted.

Intrinse, *adj*. tightly drawn.

Invised, *adj*. unseen, a doubtful word.

Irregulous, *adj*. lawless.

Jack, *sb*. figure that struck the bell in old clocks. R III. IV. 2. 114.
    A term of contempt. R III. I. 3. 72. The small bowl aimed at
    in the game of bowls. Cym. II. 1. 2. The key of a virginal.
    Sonn. CXXVIII. 5. A drinking vessel. T. of S. IV. 1. 48.

Jade, *v.t.* to play the jade with, run away with. Tw.N. II. 5.
    164. Drive like a jade. A. & C. III. 1. 34. Treat with
    contempt. H VIII. III. 2. 280.

Jakes, *sb*. a privy.

Jar, *sb*. a tick of the clock. W.T. I. 2. 43.

Jar, *v.t.* to tick. R II. V. 5. 51. *v.i.* to guard. 1 H VI. III. 1. 70.
    sb. a quarrel. 1 H VI. I. 1. 44.

Jesses, *sb*. straps attaching the legs of a hawk to the fist.

Jet, *v.i.* to strut. Tw.N. II. 4. 32. Advance threateningly. R
    III. II. 4. 51.

Journal, *adj*. diurnal, daily.

Jowl, *v.t.* to knock, dash.

Kam, *adj*. crooked, away from the point.

Keech, *sb*. a lump of tallow or fat.

Keel, *v.t.* to cool.

Ken, *sb*. perception, sight. *v.t.* to know.

Kern, *sb*. light-armed foot-soldier of Ireland.

Kibe, *sb*. chilblain on the heel.

Kicky-wicky, *sb*. a pet name.

Killen = to kill.

Kiln-hole, *sb*. the fireplace of an oven or kiln.

Kind, *sb.* nature. M. of V. I. 3. 84. *adj.* natural. Lucr. 1423. *adv.* kindly. Tim. I. 2. 224.

Kindle, *v.t.* to bring forth young. As III. 2. 343. Incite. As I. 1. 179.

Knack, *sb.* a pretty trifle.

Knap, *v.t.* to gnaw, nibble. M. of V. III. 1. 9. Rap. Lear, II. 4. 123.

Laboursome, *adj.* elaborate.

Laced mutton, *sb.* slang for courtesan.

Lade, *v.t.* to empty, drain.

Land-damn. Unrecognizably corrupt word in W.T. II. 1. 143.

Lapsed, *p.p.* caught, surprised. Tw.N. III. 3. 36.

Latch, *v.t.* to catch, lay hold of.

Latten, *sb.* a mixture of copper and tin. M.W.W. I. 1. 153.

Laund, *sb.* glade.

Lavolt, *sb.* a dance in which two persons bound high and whirl round.

Lay for, *v.t.* to strive to win.

Leasing, *sb.* lying, falsehood.

Leave, *sb.* liberty, license.

Leer, *sb.* complexion.

Leese, *v.t.* to lose.

Leet, *sb.* a manor court. T. of S. Ind. II. 87. The time when such is held. Oth. III. 3. 140.

Leiger, *sb.* ambassador.

Length, *sb.* delay.

Let, *v.t.* to hinder. Tw.N. V. 1. 246; Ham. I. 4. 85. Detain. W.T. I. 2. 41. Forbear. Lucr. 10. *p.p.* caused. Ham. IV. 6. 11. *sb.* hindrance. H V. V. 2. 65.

Let-alone, *sb.* hindrance, prohibition.

Level, *sb.* aim, line of fire. R. & J. III. 3. 102. *v.i.* to aim. R III. IV. 4. 202. Be on the same level. Oth. I. 3. 239. *adv.* evenly. Tw.N. II. 4. 32.

Lewd, *adj.* base, vile.

Libbard, *sb.* leopard.

Liberal, *adj.* licentious. Liberal conceit = elaborate design. Ham. V. 2. 152. *adv.* freely, openly. Oth. V. 2. 220.

Lieger, *sb.* ambassador.

Lifter, *sb.* thief.

Light, *p.p.* lighted.

Likelihood, *sb.* sign, indication.

Lime, *v.t.* to put lime into liquor. M.W.W. I. 3. 14. Smear with bird-lime. 2 H VI. I. 3. 86. Catch with bird-lime. Tw.N. III. 4. 75. Cement. 3 H VI. V. 1. 84.

Limit, *sb.* appointed time. R II. I. 3. 151. *v.t.* to appoint. John. V. 2. 123.

Line, *v.t.* to draw, paint. As III. 2. 93. Strengthen, fortify. 1 H IV. II. 3. 85.

Line-grove, *sb.* a grove of lime trees.

Linsey-woolsey, *sb.* gibberish (literally, mixed stuff).

Lipsbury pinfold. Perhaps = between the teeth.

List, *sb.* desire, inclination. Oth. II. 1. 105. Limit, boundary. 1 H IV. IV. I. 51. Lists for combat. Mac. III. 1. 70.

Lither, *adj.* flexible, gentle.

Livery, *sb.* delivery of a freehold into the possession of the heir.

Lob, *sb.* lubber, lout.

Lockram, *sb.* coarse linen.

Lodge, *v.t.* to lay flat, beat down.

Loggats, *sb.* a game somewhat resembling bowls.

Loof, *v.t.* to luff, bring close to the wind.

Losel, *sb.* a wasteful, worthless fellow.

Lout, *v.t.* to make a lout or fool of.

Lown, *sb.* base fellow.

Luce, *sb.* pike or jack.

Lurch, *v.t.* to win a love set at a game; bear off the prize easily. Cor. II. 2. 102. *v.i.* to skulk. M. W. W. II. 2. 25.

Lym, *sb.* bloodhound; so called from the leam or leash used to hold him.

Maggot-pie, *sb.* magpie.

Main, *sb.* a call at dice. 1 H IV. IV. 1. 47. Mainland. Lear, III. 1. 6. The chief power. Ham. V. 4. 15.

Main-course, *sb.* mainsail.

Main'd, *p.p.* maimed.

Makeless, *adj.* mateless, widowed.

Malkin, *sb.* slattern.

Mallard, *sb.* a wild drake.

Mallecho, *sb.* mischief (Span. *malhecho*).

Malt-horse, *sb.* brewer's horse.

Mammering, *pr.p.* hesitating.

Mammet, *sb.* a doll.

Mammock, *v.t.* to tear in pieces.

Manakin, *sb.* little man.

Mankind, *adj.* masculine, applied to a woman.

Manner, with the = in the act, red-handed.

Mare, *sb.* nightmare. To ride the wild mare = play at see-saw.

Mark, *sb.* thirteen shillings and fourpence.

Mart, *v.i.* to market, traffic. Cym. I. 6. 150. *v.t.* to vend, traffic with. J. C. IV. 3. 11.

Mastic, *sb.* used to stop decayed teeth.

Match, *sb.* compact, bargain. M. of V. III. 1. 40. Set a match = make an appointment. 1 H IV. 1. 2. 110.

Mate, *v.t.* to confound, make bewildered. C. of E. III. 2. 54. Match, cope with. H VIII. III. 2. 274.

Material, *adj.* full of matter.

Maugre, *prep.* in spite of.

Maund, *sb.* a basket.

Mazard, *sb.* skull.

Meacock, *adj.* spiritless, pusillanimous.

Mealed. *p.p.* mingled, compounded.

Mean, *sb.* the intermediate part between the tenor and treble.

Meiny, *sb.* attendants, retinue.

Mell, *v.i.* to meddle.

Mered, He being the mered question—the question concerning him alone. A. & C. III. 13. 10.

Mess, *sb,* a set of four. L.L.L. IV. 3. 204. Small quantity. 2 H IV. II. 1. 95. Lower messes = inferiors, as messing at the lower end of the table. W.T. I. 2. 226.

Mete, *v. i.* to mete at = aim at.

Metheglin, *sb.* a kind of mead, made of honey and water.

Micher, *sb.* truant.

Miching, *adj.* sneaking, stealthy.

Mineral, *sb.* a mine.

Minikin, *adj.* small, pretty.

Minion, *sb.* darling, favourite. John, II. 1. 392. Used contemptuously. 2 H VI. I. 3. 82. A pert, saucy person. 2 H VI. I. 3. 136.

Mirable, *adj.* admirable.

Mire, *v.i.* to be bemired, sink as into mire.

Misdread, *sb.* fear of evil.

Misprision, *sb.* mistake. M.N.D. III. 2. 90. Contempt. A.W. II. 3. 153.

Misproud, *adj.* viciously proud.

Miss, *sb.* misdoing.

Missingly, *adv.* regretfully.

Missive, *sb.* messenger.

Misthink, *v.t.* to misjudge.

Mobled, *p.p.* having the face or head muffled.

Modern, *adj.* commonplace, trite.

Module, *sb.* mould, form.

Moldwarp, *sb.* mole.

Mome, *sb.* blockhead, dolt.

Momentany, *adj.* momentary, lasting an instant.

Monster, *v.t.* to make monstrous.

Month's mind, *sb.* intense desire or yearning.

Moralize, *v.t.* to interpret, explain.

Mort, *sb.* trumpet notes blown at the death of the deer.

Mortal, *adj.* deadly.

Mortified, *p.p.* deadened, insensible.

Mot, *sb.* motto, device.

Mother, *sb.* the disease *hysterica passio*.

Motion, *v.t.* to propose, counsel. 1 H VI. I. 3. 63. *sb.* a puppet show. W.T. IV. 3. 96. A puppet. Two G. II. 1. 91. Solicitation, proposal, suit. C. of E. I. 1. 60. Emotion, feeling, impulse. Tw.N. II. 4. 18.

Motive, *sb*. a mover, instrument, member.

Mountant, *adj*. lifted up.

Mow, *sb*. a grimace. *v.i.* to grimace.

Moy, *sb*. probably some coin.

Muleter, *sb*. *muleteer*.

Mulled, *p.p.* flat, insipid.

Mummy, *sb*. a medical or magical preparation originally made from mummies.

Murdering-piece, *sb*. a cannon loaded with chain-shot.

Murrion, *adj*. infected with the murrain.

Muse, *v.i.* to wonder. John, III. 1. 317. *v.t.* to wonder at. Tp. III. 3. 36.

Muset, *sb*. a gap or opening in a hedge.

Muss, *sb*. scramble.

Mutine, *sb*. mutineer.

Mystery, *sb*. profession. M. for M. IV. 2. 28. Professional skill. A.W. III. 6. 65.

Nayword, *sb*. pass-word, M.W.W. II. 2. 126. A by-word. Tw.N. II. 3. 132.

Neat, *adj*. trim, spruce.

Neb, *sb*. bill or beak.

Neeld, *sb*. needle.

Neeze, *v.i.* to sneeze.

Neif, *sb*. fist.

Next, *adj*. nearest.

Nick, *sb*. out of all nick, beyond all reckoning.

Night-rule, *sb*. revelry.

Nill = will not.

Nine-men's-morris, *sb*. a rustic game.

Note, *sb*. list, catalogue. W.T. IV. 2. 47. Note of expectation = list of expected guests. Mac. III. 3. 10. Stigma, mark of reproach. R II. 1. 1. 43. Distinction. Cym. II. 3. 12. knowledge, observation. Lear, III. 1. 18.

Nott-pated, *adj*. crop-headed.

Nousle, *v.t.* to nurse, nourish delicately.

Nowl, *sb*. noddle.

Nuthook, *sb.* slang for catchpole.

Oathable, *adj.* capable of taking an oath.

Object, *sb.* anything presented to the sight; everything that comes in the way.

Obsequious, *adj.* regardful of funeral rites. 3 H VI. II. 5. 118. Funereal, having to do with obsequies. T. A. V. 3. 153.

Observance, *sb.* observation. Oth. III. 3. 151. Homage. 2 H IV. IV. 3. 15. Ceremony. M. of V. II. 2. 194.

Obstacle, *sb.* blunder for obstinate.

Occupation, *sb.* trade (in contemptuous sense). Cor. IV. 1. 14. Voice of occupation = vote of working men. Cor. IV. 6. 98.

Odd, *adj.* unnoticed. Tp. I. 2. 223. At odds. T. & C. IV. 5. 265.

Oeillades, *sb.* amorous glances.

O' ergrown, *p.p.* bearded. Cym. IV. 4. 33. Become too old. M. for M. I. 3. 22.

O'erstrawed, *p.p.* overstrewn.

Office, *v.t.* to office all = do all the domestic service. A. W. III. 2. 128. Keep officiously. Cor. V. 2. 61.

Oneyers, *sb.* unexplained word.

Opposition, *sb.* combat, encounter.

Orb, *sb.* orbit. R. & J. II. 1. 151. Circle. M.N.D. II. 1. 9. A heavenly body. M. of V. V. 1. 60. The earth. Tw.N. III. 1. 39.

Ordinant, *adj.* ordaining, controlling.

Ordinary, *sb.* a public dinner at which each man pays for his own share.

Ort, *sb.* remnant, refuse.

Ouphs, *sb.* elves, goblins.

Outrage, *sb.* outburst of rage.

Overscutch'd, *p.p.* over-whipped, over-switched (perhaps in a wanton sense).

Overture, *sb.* disclosure. W.T. II. 1. 172. Declaration. Tw.N. I. 5. 208.

Owe, *v.t.* to own, possess.

Packing, *sb.* plotting, conspiracy.

Paddock, *sb.* toad. Ham. III. 4. 191. A familiar spirit in the form of a toad. Mac. I. 1. 9.

Pajock, *sb.* term of contempt, by some said to mean peacock.

Pale, *sb.* enclosure, confine.

Palliament, *sb.* robe.

Parcel-bawd, *sb.* half-bawd.

Paritor, *sb.* apparitor, an officer of the Bishops' Court.

Part, *sb.* party, side.

Partake, *v.t.* to make to partake, impart. W.T. V. 3. 132. To share. J.C. II. 1. 305.

Parted, *p.p.* endowed.

Partisan, *sb.* a kind of pike.

Pash, *sb.* a grotesque word for the head. W.T. I. 2. 128. *v.t.* to smite, dash. T. & C. II. 3. 202.

Pass, *v.t.* to pass sentence on. M. for M. II. 1. 19. Care for. 2 H VI. IV. 2. 127. Represent. L.L.L. V. 1. 123. Make a thrust in fencing. Tw.N. III. 1. 44.

Passage, *sb.* passing to and fro. C. of E. III. 1. 99. Departure, death. Ham. III. 3. 86. Passing away. 1 H VI. II. 5. 108. Occurrence. A.W. I. 1. 19. Process, course. R. & J. Prol. 9. Thy passages of life = the actions of thy life. 1 H IV. III. 2. 8. Passages of grossness = gross impositions. Tw.N. III. 2. 70. Motion. Cor. V. 6. 76.

Passant. In heraldry, the position of an animal walking.

Passion, *sb.* passionate poem. M.N.D. V. 1. 306; Sonn. XX. 2.

Passionate, *v.t.* to express with emotion. T.A. III. 2. 6. *adj.* displaying emotion. 2 H VI. I. 1. 104. Sorrowful. John, II. 1. 544.

Passy measures, a corruption of the Italian *passamezzo*, denoting a stately and measured step in dancing.

Patch, *sb.* fool.

Patchery, *sb.* knavery, trickery.

Patronage, *v.t.* to patronize, protect.

Pavin, *sb.* a stately dance of Spanish or Italian origin.

Pawn, *sb.* a pledge.

Peach, *v.t.* to impeach, accuse.

Peat, *sb.* pet, darling.

Pedascule, *sb.* vocative, pedant, schoolmaster.

Peevish, *adj.* childish, silly. 1 H VI. V. 3. 186. Fretful, wayward. M. of V. I. 1. 86.

Peise, *v.t.* to poise, balance. John, II. 1. 575. Retard by making heavy. M. of V. III. 2. 22. Weigh down. R III. V. 3. 106.

Pelt, *v.i.* to let fly with words of opprobrium.

Pelting, *adj.* paltry.

Penitent, *adj.* doing penance.

Periapt, *sb.* amulet.

Period, *sb.* end, conclusion. A. & C. IV. 2. 25. *v.t.* to put an end to. Tim. I. 1. 103.

Perked up, *p.p.* dressed up.

Perspective, *sb.* glasses so fashioned as to create an optical illusion.

Pert, *adj.* lively, brisk.

Pertaunt-like, *adv.* word unexplained and not yet satisfactorily amended. L.L.L. V. 2. 67.

Pervert, *v.t.* to avert, turn aside.

Pettitoes, *sb.* feet; properly pig's feet.

Pheeze, *v.t.* beat, chastise, torment.

Phisnomy, *sb.* physiognomy.

Phraseless, *adj.* indescribable.

Physical, *adj.* salutary, wholesome.

Pia mater, *sb.* membrane that covers the brain; used for the brain itself.

Pick, *v.t.* to pitch, throw.

Picked, *p.p.* refined, precise.

Picking, *adj.* trifling, small.

Piece, *sb.* a vessel of wine.

Pight, *p.p.* pitched.

Piled, *p.p* = peeled, bald, with quibble on 'piled' of velvet.

Pill, *v.t.* to pillage, plunder.

Pin, *sb.* bull's-eye of a target.

Pin-buttock, *sb.* a narrow buttock.

Pioned, *adj.* doubtful word: perhaps covered with marsh-marigold, or simply dug.

Pip, *sb.* a spot on cards. A pip out = intoxicated, with reference to a game called one and thirty.

Pitch, *sb.* the height to which a falcon soars, height.

Placket, *sb.* opening in a petticoat, or a petticoat.

Planched, *adj.* made of planks.

Plantage, *sb.* plants, vegetation.

Plantation, *sb.* colonizing.

Plausive, *adj.* persuasive, pleasing.

Pleached, *adj.* interlaced, folded.

Plurisy, *sb.* superabundance.

Point-devise, *adj.* precise, finical. L.L.L. V. 1.19. *adv.* Tw.N. II. 5. 162.

Poking-sticks, *sb.* irons for setting out ruffs.

Pole-clipt, *adj.* used of vineyards in which the vines are grown around poles.

Polled, *adj.* clipped, laid bare.

Pomander, *sb.* a ball of perfume.

Poor-John, *sb.* salted and dried hake.

Porpentine, *sb.* porcupine.

Portable, *adj.* supportable, endurable.

Portage, *sb.* port-hole. H V. III. 1. 10. Port-dues. Per. III. 1. 35.

Portance, *sb.* deportment, bearing.

Posse, *v.t.* to curdle.

Posy, *sb.* a motto on a ring.

Potch, *v.i.* to poke, thrust.

Pottle, *sb.* a tankard; strictly a two quart measure.

Pouncet-box, *sb.* a box for perfumes, pierced with holes.

Practice, *sb.* plot.

Practisant, *sb.* accomplice.

Practise, *v.i.* to plot, use stratagems. Two G. IV. 1. 47. *v.t.* to plot. John, IV. 1. 20.

Precedent, *sb.* rough draft. R III. III. 6. 7. Prognostic, indication. V. & A. 26.

Prefer, *v.t.* to promote, advance. Two G. II. 4. 154. Recommend. Cym. II. 3. 50. Present offer. M.N.D. IV. 2. 37.

Pregnant, *adj.* ready-witted, clever. Tw.N. II. 2. 28. Full of meaning. Ham. II. 2. 209. Ready. Ham. III. 2. 66. Plain, evident. M. for M. II. 1. 23.

Prenzie, *adj.* demure.

Pretence, *sb.* project, scheme.

Prick, *sb.* point on a dial. 3 H VI. I. 4. 34. Bull's-eye. L.L.L. IV. 1. 132. Prickle. As III. 2. 113. Skewer. Lear, II. 3. 16.

Pricket, *sb.* a buck of the second year.

Prick-song, *sb.* music sung from notes.

Prig, *sb.* a thief.

Private, *sb.* privacy. Tw.N. III. 4. 90. Private communication. John, IV. 3. 16.

Prize, *sb.* prize-contest. T.A. I. 1. 399. Privilege. 3 H VI. I. 4. 59. Value. Cym. III. 6. 76.

Probal, *adj.* probable, reasonable.

Proditor, *sb.* traitor.

Proface, *int.* much good may it do you!

Propagate, *v.t.* to augment.

Propagation, *sb.* augmentation.

Proper-false, *adj.* handsome and deceitful.

Property, *sb.* a tool or instrument. M.W.W. III. 4. 10. *v.t.* to make a tool of. John, V. 2. 79.

Pugging, *adj.* thievish.

Puisny, *adj.* unskilful, like a tyro.

Pun, *v.t.* to pound.

Punk, *sb.* strumpet.

Purchase, *v.t.* to acquire, get. *sb.* acquisition, booty.

Pursuivant, *sb.* a herald's attendant or messenger.

Pursy, *adj.* short-winded, asthmatic.

Puttock, *sb.* a kite.

Puzzel, *sb.* a filthy drab (Italian *puzzolente*).

Quaintly, *adv.* ingeniously, deliberately.

Qualification, *sb.* appeasement.

Quality, *sb.* profession, calling, especially that of an actor. Two G. IV. I. 58. Professional skill. Tp. I. 2. 193.

Quarter, *sb.* station. John, V. 5. 20. Keep fair quarter = keep on good terms with, be true to. C. of E. II. I. 108. In quarter = on good terms. Oth. II. 3. 176.

Quat, *sb.* pimple.

Quatch-buttock, *sb.* a squat or flat buttock.

Quean, *sb.* wench, hussy.

Queasiness, *sb.* nausea, disgust.

Queasy, *adj.* squeamish, fastidious. M.A. II. I. 368. Disgusted. A. & C. III. 6. 20.

Quell, *sb.* murder.

Quest, *sb.* inquest, jury. R III. I. 4. 177. Search, inquiry, pursuit. M. of V. I. 1. 172. A body of searchers. Oth. I. 2. 46.

Questant, *sb.* aspirant, candidate.

Quicken, *v.t.* to make alive. A.W. II. I. 76. Refresh, revive. M. of V. II. 7. 52. *v.i.* to become alive, revive. Lear, III. 7. 40.

Quietus, *sb.* settlement of an account.

Quill, *sb.* body. 2 H VI. I. 3. 3.

Quillet, *sb.* quibble.

Quintain, *sb.* a figure set up for tilting at.

Quire, *sb.* company.

Quittance, *v.i.* to requite. I H VI. II. I. 14. *sb.* acquittance. M. W. W. I. I. 10. Requital. 2 H IV. I. I. 108.

Quoif, *sb.* cap.

Quoit, *v.t.* to throw.

Quote, *v.t.* to note, examine.

Rabato, *sb.* a kind of ruff.

Rabbit-sucker, *sb.* sucking rabbit.

Race, *sb.* root. W.T. IV. 3. 48. Nature, disposition. M. for M. II. 4. 160. Breed. Mac. II. 4. 15.

Rack, *v.t.* stretch, strain. M. of V. I. 1. 181. Strain to the utmost. *Cor.* V. 1. 16.

Rack, *sb.* a cloud or mass of clouds. Ham. II. 2. 492. *v.i.* move like vapour. 3 H VI. II. 1. 27.

Rampired, *p.p.* fortified by a rampart.

Ramps, *sb.* wanton wenches.

Ranges, *sb.* ranks.

Rap, *v.t.* to transport.

Rascal, *sb.* a deer out of condition.

Raught, *impf.* & *p.p.* reached.

Rayed, *p.p.* befouled. T. of S. IV. 1. 3. In T. of S. III. 2. 52 it perhaps means arrayed, *i.e.* attacked.

Raze, *sb.* root.

Razed, *p.p.* slashed.

Reave, *v.t.* to bereave.

Rebate, *v.t.* to make dull, blunt.

Recheat, *sb.* a set of notes sounded to call hounds off a false scent.

Rede, *sb.* counsel.

Reechy, *adj.* smoky, grimy.

Refell, *v.t.* to refute.

Refuse, *sb.* rejection, disowning. *v.t.* to reject, disown.

Reguerdon, *v.t.* to reward, guerdon.

Remonstrance, *sb.* demonstration.

Remotion, *sb.* removal.

Renege, *v.t.* to deny.

Renying, *pres. p.* denying.

Replication, *sb.* echo. J.C. I. 1. 50. Reply. Ham. IV. 2. 12.

Rere-mice, *sb.* bats.

Respected, blunder for suspected.

Respective, *adj.* worthy of regard. Two G. IV. 4. 197. Showing regard. John, I. 1. 188. Careful. M. of V. V. 1. 156.

Respectively, *adv.* respectfully.

Rest, *sb.* set up one's rest is to stand upon the cards in one's hand, be fully resolved.

Resty, *adj.* idle, lazy.

Resume, *v.t.* to take.

Reverb, *v.t.* to resound.

Revolt, *sb.* rebel.

Ribaudred, *adj.* ribald, lewd.

Rid, *v.t.* to destroy, do away with.

Riggish, *adj*. wanton.

Rigol, *sb*. a circle.

Rim, *sb*. midriff or abdomen.

Rivage, *sb*. shore.

Rival, *sb*. partner, companion. M.N.D. III. 2. 156. *v.i.* to be a competitor. Lear, I. 1. 191.

Rivality, *sb*. partnership, participation.

Rivelled, *adj*. wrinkled.

Road, *sb*. roadstead, port. Two G. 11. 4. 185. Journey. H VIII. IV. 2. 17. Inroad, incursion. H V. I. 2. 138.

Roisting, *adj*. roistering, blustering.

Romage, *sb*. bustle, turmoil.

Ronyon, *sb*. scurvy wretch.

Rook, *v.i.* to cower, squat.

Ropery, *sb*. roguery.

Rope-tricks, *sb*. knavish tricks.

Roping, *pr.p.* dripping.

Roted, *p.p.* learned by heart.

Rother, *sb*. an ox, or animal of the ox kind.

Round, *v.i.* to whisper. John, II. 1. 566. *v.t.* to surround. M.N.D. IV. 1. 52.

Round, *adj*. straightforward, blunt, plainspoken. C. of E. II. 1. 82.

Rouse, *sb*. deep draught, bumper.

Rout, *sb*. crowd, mob. C. of E. III. 1. 101. Brawl. Oth. II. 3. 210.

Row, *sb*. verse or stanza.

Roynish, *adj*. scurvy; hence coarse, rough.

Rub, *v.i.* to encounter obstacles. L.L.L. IV. 1. 139. Rub on, of a bowl that surmounts the obstacle in its course. T. & C. III. 2. 49. *sb*. impediment, hindrance; from the game of bowls. John, III. 4. 128.

Ruffle, *v.i.* to swagger, bully. T.A. I. 1. 314.

Ruddock, *sb*. the redbreast.

Rudesby, *sb*. a rude fellow.

Rump-fed, *adj*. pampered; perhaps fed on offal, or else fat-rumped.

Running banquet, a hasty refreshment (fig.).

Rush aside, *v.t.* to pass hasitily by, thrust aside.

Rushling, blunder for rustling.

Sad, *adj.* grave, serious. M. of V. II. 2. 195. Gloomy, sullen. R II. V. 5. 70.

Sagittary, *sb.* a centaur. T. & C. V. 5. 14. The official residence in the arsenal at Venice. Oth. I. 1. 160.

Sallet, *sb.* a close-fitting helmet. 2 H VI. IV. 10. 11. A salad. 2 H VI. IV. 10. 8.

Salt, *sb.* salt-cellar. Two G. III. 1. 354. *adj.* lecherous. M. for M. V. 1. 399. Stinging, bitter. T. & C. I. 3. 371.

Salutation, *sb.* give salutation to my blood = make my blood rise.

Salute, *v.t.* to meet. John, II. 1. 590. To affect. H VIII. II. 3. 103.

Sanded, *adj.* sandy-coloured.

Say, *sb.* a kind of silk.

Scald, *adj.* scurvy, scabby. H V. V. 1. 5.

Scale, *v.t.* to put in the scales, weigh.

Scall = scald. M.W.W. III. 1. 115.

Scamble, *v.i.* to scramble.

Scamel, *sb.* perhaps a misprint for seamell, or seamew.

Scantling, *sb.* a scanted or small portion.

Scape, *sb.* freak, escapade.

Sconce, *sb.* a round fort. H V. III. 6. 73. Hence a protection for the head. C. of E. II. 2. 37. Hence the skull. Ham. V. 1. 106. *v.r.* to ensconce, hide. Ham. III. 4. 4.

Scotch, *sb.* notch. *v.t.* to cut, slash.

Scrowl, *v.i.* perhaps for to scrawl.

Scroyles, *sb.* scabs, scrofulous wretches.

Scrubbed, *adj.* undersized.

Scull, *sb.* shoal of fish.

Seal, *sb.* to give seals = confirm, carry out.

Seam, *sb.* grease, lard.

Seconds, *sb.* an inferior kind of flour.

Secure, *adj.* without care, confident.

Security, *sb.* carelessness, want of caution.

Seedness, *sb.* sowing with seed.

Seel, *v.t.* to close up a hawk's eyes.

Self-admission, *sb.* self-approbation.

Semblative, *adj.* resembling, like.

Sequestration, *sb.* separation.

Serpigo, *sb.* tetter or eruption on the skin.

Sessa, *int.* exclamation urging to speed.

Shard-borne, *adj.* borne through the air on shards.

Shards, *sb.* the wing cases of beetles. A. & C. III. 2. 20. Potsherds. Ham. V. 1. 254.

Sharked up, *p.p.* gathered indiscriminately.

Shealed, *p.p.* shelled.

Sheep-biter, *sb.* a malicious, niggardly fellow.

Shent, *p.p.* scolded, rebuked. M.W.W. I. 4. 36.

Shive, *sb.* slice.

Shog, *v.i.* to move, jog.

Shore, *sb.* a sewer.

Shrewd, *adj.* mischievous, bad.

Shrewdly, *adv.* badly.

Shrewdness, *sb.* mischievousness.

Shrieve, *sb.* sheriff.

Shrowd, *sb.* shelter, protection.

Siege, *sb.* seat. M. for M. IV. 2. 98. Rank. Ham. IV. 7. 75. Excrement. Tp. II. 2. 111.

Significant, *sb.* sign, token.

Silly, *adj.* harmless, innocent. Two G. IV. 1. 72. Plain, simple. Tw.N. II. 4. 46.

Simular, *adj.* simulated, counterfeited. Cym. V. 5. 20. *sb.* simulator, pretender. Lear, III. 2. 54.

Sitch, *adv.* and *conj.* since.

Skains-mates, *sb.* knavish companions.

Slab, *adj.* slabby, slimy.

Sleeve-hand, *sb.* wristband.

Sleided, *adj.* untwisted.

Slipper, *adj.* slippery.

Slobbery, *adj.* dirty.

Slubber, *v.t.* to slur over, do carelessly.

Smatch, *sb.* smack, taste.

Sneak-cup, *sb.* a fellow who shirks his liquor.

Sneap, *v.t.* to pinch, nip. L.L.L. I. 1. 100. *sb.* snub, reprimand. 2 H IV. II. 1. 125.

Sneck up, contemptuous expression = go and be hanged.

Snuff, *sb.* quarrel. Lear, III. 1. 26. Smouldering wick of a candle. Cym. I. 6. 87. Object of contempt. A.W. I. 2. 60. Take in snuff = take offence at. L.L.L. V. 2. 22.

Sob, *sb.* a rest given to a horse to regain its wind.

Solidare, *sb.* a small coin.

Sonties, *sb.* corruption of saints.

Sooth, *sb.* flattery.

Soothers, *sb.* flatterers.

Sophy, *sb.* the Shah of Persia.

Sore, *sb.* a buck of the fourth year.

Sorel, *sb.* a buck of the third year.

Sort, *sb.* rank. M.A. I. 1. 6. Set, company. R III. V. 3. 316. Manner. M. of V. I. 2. 105. Lot. T. & C. I. 3. 376.

Sort, *v.t.* to pick out. Two G. III. 2. 92. To rank. Ham. II. 2. 270. To arrange, dispose. R III. II. 2. 148. To adapt. 2 H VI. II. 4. 68. *v.i.* to associate. V. & A. 689. To be fitting. T. & C. I. 1. 109. Fall out, happen. M.N.D. III. 2. 352.

Souse, *v.t.* to swoop down on, as a falcon.

Sowl, *v.t.* to lug, drag by the ears.

Span-counter, *sb.* boy's game of throwing a counter so as to strike, or rest within a span of, an opponent's counter.

Speed, *sb.* fortune, success.

Speken = speak.

Sperr, *v.t.* to bar.

Spital, *sb.* hospital.

Spital house, *sb.* hospital.

Spleen, *sb.* quick movement. M.N.D. I. 1. 146. Fit of laughter. L.L.L. III. 1. 76.

Spot, *sb.* pattern in embroidery.

Sprag, *adj.* sprack, quick, lively.

Spring, *sb.* a young shoot.

Springhalt, *sb.* a lameness in horses.

Spurs, *sb.* the side roots of a tree.

Squandering, *adj.* roving, random. As II. 7. 57.

Square, *sb.* the embroidery about the bosom of a smock or shift. W.T. IV. 3. 212. Most precious square of sense = the most sensitive part. Lear, I. 1. 74.

Square, *v.i.* to quarrel.

Squash, *sb.* an unripe peascod.

Squier, *sb.* square, rule.

Squiny, *v.i.* to look asquint.

Staggers, *sb.* giddiness, bewilderment. A.W. II. 3. 164. A disease of horses. T. of S. III. 2. 53.

Stale, *sb.* laughing stock, dupe. 3 H VI. III. 3. 260. Decoy. T. of S. III. 1. 90. Stalking-horse. C. of E. II. 1. 101. Prostitute. M.A. II. 2. 24. Horse-urine. A. & C. I. 4. 62.

Stamp, *v.t.* to mark as genuine, give currency to.

Standing, *sb.* duration, continuance. W.T. I. 2. 430. Attitude. Tim. I. 1. 34.

Standing-tuck, *sb.* a rapier standing on end.

Staniel, *sb.* a hawk, the kestrel.

Stare, *v.i.* to stand on end.

State, *sb.* attitude. L.L.L. IV. 3. 183. A chair of state. 1 H IV. II. 4. 390. Estate, fortune. M. of V. III. 2. 258. States (pl.) = persons of high position. John, II. 1. 395.

Statute-caps, *sb.* woollen caps worn by citizens as decreed by the Act of 1571.

Staves, *sb.* shafts of lances.

Stead, *v.t.* to help.

Stead up, *v.t.* to take the place of.

Stelled, *p.p.* fixed. Lucr. 1444. Sonn. XXIV. 1. Starry. Lear, III. 7. 62.

Stickler-like, *adj.* like a stickler, whose duty it was to separate combatants.

Stigmatic, *adj.* marked by deformity.

Stillitory, *sb.* a still.

Stint, *v.i.* to stop, cease. R. & J. I. 3. 48. *v.t.* to check, stop. T. & C. IV. 5. 93.

Stock, *sb.* a dowry. Two G. III. 1. 305. A stocking. Two G. III. 1. 306; 1 H IV. II. 4. 118. A thrust in fencing. M.W.W. II. 3. 24. *v.t.* to put in the stocks. Lear, II. 2. 333.

Stomach, *sb.* courage. 2 H IV. I. 1. 129. Pride. T. of S. V. 2. 177.

Stomaching, *sb.* resentment.

Stone-bow, *sb.* a cross-bow for shooting stones.

Stoop, *sb.* a drinking vessel.

Stricture, *sb.* strictness.

Stride, *v.t.* to overstep.

Stover, *sb.* cattle fodder.

Stuck, *sb.* a thrust in fencing.

Subject, *sb.* subjects, collectively.

Subscribe, *v.i.* to be surety. A.W. III. 6. 84. Yield, submit. 1 H VI. II. 4. 44. *v.t.* to admit, acknowledge. M.A. V. 2. 58.

Subtle, *adj.* deceptively smooth.

Successantly, *adv.* in succession.

Sufferance, *sb.* suffering. M. for M. II. 2. 167. Patience. M. of V. I. 3. 109. Loss. Oth. II. 1. 23. Death penalty. H V. II. 2. 158.

Suggest, *v.t.* to tempt.

Suit, *sb.* service, attendance. M. for M. IV. 4. 19. Out of suits with fortune = out of fortune's service.

Supervise, *sb.* inspection.

Suppliance, *sb.* pastime.

Sur-addition, *sb.* an added title.

Surmount, *v.i.* to surpass, exceed. 1 H VI. V. 3. 191. *v.t.* to surpass. L.L.L. V. 2. 677.

Sur-reined, *p.p.* overridden.

Suspect, *sb.* suspicion.

Swarth, *adj.* black. T.A. II. 3. 71. *sb.* swath. Tw.N. II. 3. 145.

Swoopstake, *adv.* in one sweep, wholesale.

Tag, *sb.* rabble.

Take, *v.t.* to captivate. W.T. IV. 3. 119. Strike. M.W.W. IV. 4. 32. Take refuge in. C. of E. V. 1. 36. Leap over. John,

V. 2. 138. Take in = conquer. A. & C. I. 1 .23. Take out = copy. Oth. III. 3. 296. Take thought = feel grief for. J.C. II. 1. 187. Take up = get on credit. 2 H VI. IV. 7. 125. Reconcile. Tw.N. III. 4. 294. Rebuke. Two G. I. 2. 134.

Tallow-keech, *sb.* a vessel filled with tallow.

Tanling, *sb.* one tanned by the sun. John, IV. 1. 117. Incite. Ham. II. 2. 358.

Tarre, *v.t.* to set on dogs to fight.

Taste, *sb.* trial, proof. *v.t.* to try, prove.

Tawdry-lace, *sb.* a rustic necklace.

Taxation, *sb.* satire, censure. As I. 2. 82. Claim, demand. Tw.N. I. 5. 210.

Teen, *sb.* grief.

Tenable, *adj.* capable of being kept.

Tend, *v.i.* to wait, attend. Ham. I. 3. 83. Be attentive. Tp. I. 1. 6. *v.t.* to tend to, regard. 2 H VI. I. 1. 204. Wait upon. A. & C. II. 2. 212.

Tendance, *sb.* attention. Tim. I. 1. 60. Persons attending. Tim. I. 1. 74.

Tender, *v.t.* to hold dear, regard. R III. I. 1. 44. *sb.* care, regard. 1 H IV. V. 4. 49.

Tender-hefted, *adj.* set in a delicate handle or frame.

Tent, *sb.* probe. T. & C. II. 2. 16. *v.t.* to probe. Ham. II. 2. 608. Cure. Cor. I. 9. 31.

Tercel, *sb.* male goshawk.

Termless, *adj.* not to be described.

Testerned, *p.p.* presented with sixpence.

Testril, *sb.* sixpence.

Tetchy, *adj.* irritable.

Tetter, *sb.* skin erruption. Ham. I. 5. 71. *v.t.* to infect with tetter. Cor. III. 1. 99.

Than = then, Lucr. 1440.

Tharborough, *sb.* third borough, constable.

Thick, *adv.* rapidly, close.

Thirdborough, *sb.* constable.

Thisne, perhaps = in this way. M.N.D. I. 2. 48.

Thoughten, *p.p.* be you thoughten = entertain the thought.

Thrall, *sb.* thraldom, slavery. Pass. P. 266. *adj.* enslaved. V. & A. 837.

Three-man beetle, a rammer operated by three men.

Three-man songmen, three-part glee-singers.

Three-pile, *sb.* the finest kind of velvet.

Three-piled, *adj.* having a thick pile. M. for M. I. 2. 32. Superfine (met.). L.L.L. V. 2. 407.

Tickle, *adj.* unstable. 2 H VI. I. 1. 216. Tickle of the sere, used of lungs readily prompted to laughter; literally hair-triggered. Ham. II. 2. 329.

Ticklish, *adj.* wanton.

Tight, *adj.* swift, deft. A. & C. IV. 4. 15. Water-tight, sound. T. of S. II. 1. 372.

Tightly, *adv.* briskly, smartly.

Time-pleaser, *sb.* time server, one who complies with the times.

Tire, *sb.* headdress. Two G. IV. 4. 187. Furniture. Per II. 2. 21.

Tire, *v.i.* to feed greedily. 3 H VI. I. 1. 269. *v.t.* make to feed greedily. Lucr. 417.

Tisick, *sb.* phthisic, a cough.

Toaze, *v.t.* to draw out, untangle.

Tod, *sb.* Twenty-eight pounds of wool. *v.t.* to yield a tod.

Toged, *adj.* wearing a toga.

Toll, *v.i.* to pay toll. A.W. V. 3. 147. *v.t.* to take toll. John, III. 1. 154.

Touch, *sb.* trait. As V. 4. 27. Dash, spice. R III. IV. 4. 157. Touchstone. R III. IV. 2. 8. Of noble touch = of tried nobility. Cor. IV. 1. 49. Brave touch = fine test of valour. M.N.D. III. 2. 70. Slight hint. H VIII. V. 1. 13. Know no touch = have no skill. R II. I. 3. 165.

Touse, *v.t.* to pull, tear.

Toy, *sb.* trifle, idle fancy, folly.

Tract, *sb.* track, trace. Tim. I. 1. 53. Course. H VIII. I. 1. 40.

Train, *v.t.* to allure, decoy. 1 H VI. I. 3. 25. *sb.* bait, allurement. Mac. IV. 3. 118.

Tranect, *sb.* ferry, a doubtful word.

Translate, *v.t.* to transform.

Trash, *v.t.* lop off branches. Tp. I. 2. 81. Restrain a dog by a trash or strap. Oth. II. 1. 307.

Traverse, *v.i.* to march to the right or left.

Tray-trip, *sb.* a game at dice, which was won by throwing a trey.

Treachors, *sb.* traitors.

Treatise, *sb.* discourse.

Trench, *v.t.* to cut. Two G. III. 2. 7. Divert from its course by digging. H IV. III. 1. 112.

Troll-my-dames, *sb.* the French game of *trou madame*, perhaps akin to bagatelle.

Tropically, *adv.* figuratively.

True-penny, *sb.* an honest fellow. Ham. I. 5. 150.

Try, *sb.* trial, test. Tim. VI. 1. 9. Bring to try = bring a ship as close to the wind as possible.

Tub, *sb.* and tubfast, *sb.* a cure of venereal disease by sweating and fasting.

Tuck, *sb.* rapier.

Tun-dish, *sb.* funnel.

Turk, to turn Turk = to be a renegade. M.A. III. 4. 52. Turk Gregory = Pope Gregory VII. 1 H IV. V. 3. 125.

Twiggen, *adj.* made of twigs or wicker.

Twilled, *adj.* perhaps, covered with sedge or reeds.

Twire, *v.i.* to twinkle.

Umber, *sb.* a brown colour.

Umbered, *p.p.* made brown, darkened.

Umbrage, *sb.* a shadow.

Unaneled, *adj.* not having received extreme unction.

Unbarbed, *adj.* wearing no armour, bare.

Unbated, *adj.* unblunted.

Unbraced, *adj.* unbuttoned.

Uncape, *v.i.* to uncouple, throw off the hounds.

Uncase, *v.i.* to undress.

Unclew, *v.t.* to unwind, undo.

Uncolted, *p.p.* deprived of one's horse. 1 H IV. II. 2. 41.

Uncomprehensive, *adj.* incomprehensible.

Unconfirmed, *adj.* inexperienced.

Undercrest, *v.t.* to wear upon the crest.

Undertaker, *sb.* agent, person responsible to another for something.

Underwrite, *v.t.* to submit to.

Undistinguished, *adj.* not to be seen distinctly, unknowable.

Uneath, *adv.* hardly, with difficulty.

Unfolding, *adj.* unfolding star, the star at whose rising the shepherd lets the sheep out of the fold.

Unhappy, *adj.* mischievous, unlucky.

Unhatched, *p.p.* unhacked. Tw.N. III. 4. 234. Undisclosed. Oth. III. 4. 140.

Unhouseled, *adj.* without having received the sacrament.

Union, *sb.* large pearl.

Unkind, *adj.* unnatural. Lear, I. I. 261. Childless. V. & A. 204.

Unlived, *p.p.* deprived of life.

Unpaved, *adj.* without stones.

Unpinked, *adj.* not pinked, or pierced with eyelet holes.

Unraked, *adj.* not made up for the night.

Unrecuring, *adj.* incurable.

Unrolled, *p.p.* struck off the roll.

Unseeming, *pr.p.* not seeming.

Unseminared, *p.p.* deprived of seed or virility.

Unset, *adj.* unplanted.

Unshunned, *adj.* inevitable.

Unsifted, *adj.* untried, inexperienced.

Unsquared, *adj.* unsuitable.

Unstate, *v.t.* to deprive of dignity.

Untented, *adj.* incurable.

Unthrift, *sb.* prodigal. *adj.* good for nothing.

Untraded, *adj.* unhackneyed.

Unyoke, *v.t.* to put off the yoke, take ease after labour. Ham. V. I. 55. *v.t.* to disjoin. John, III. I. 241.

Up-cast, *sb.* a throw at bowls; perhaps the final throw.

Upshoot, *sb.* decisive shot.

Upspring, *sb.* a bacchanalian dance.

Upstaring, *adj.* standing on end.

Urchin, *sb.* hedgehog. T.A. II. 3. 101. A goblin. M.W.W. IV. 4. 49.

Usance, *sb.* interest.

Use, *sb.* interest. M.A. II. 1. 269. Usage. M. for M. I. 1. 40. In use = in trust. M. of V. IV. 1. 383.

Use, *v.r.* to behave oneself.

Uses, *sb.* manners, usages.

Utis, *sb.* boisterous merriment.

Vade, *v.i.* to fade.

Vail, *sb.* setting (of the sun). T. & C. V. 8. 7. *v.t.* to lower, let fall. 1 H VI. V. 3. 25. *v.i.* to bow. Per. IV. Prol. 29.

Vails, *sb.* a servant's perquisites.

Vain, for vain = to no purpose.

Vantbrace, *sb.* armour for the forearm.

Vast, *adj.* waste, desolate, boundless.

Vaunt-couriers, *sb.* fore-runners.

Vaward, *sb.* vanguard. 1 H VI. I. 1. 132. The first part. M.N.D. IV. 1. 106.

Vegetives, *sb.* plants.

Velvet-guards, *sb.* velvet linings, used metaphorically of those who wear them. 1 H IV. III. 1. 256.

Veney, or venew, *sb.* a fencing bout, a hit.

Venge, *v.t.* to avenge.

Vent, *sb.* discharge. Full of vent = effervescent like wine.

Via, *interj.* away, on!

Vice, *sb.* the buffoon in old morality plays. R III. III. 1. 82. *v.t.* to screw (met.) W.T. I. 2. 415.

Vinewedst, *adj.* mouldy, musty.

Violent, *v.i.* to act violently, rage.

Virginalling, *pr.p.* playing with the fingers as upon the virginals.

Virtuous, *adj.* efficacious, powerful. Oth. III. 4 .110. Essential. M.N.D. III. 2. 367. Virtuous season = benignant influence. M. for M. II. 2. 168.

Vouch, *sb.* testimony, guarantee. 1 H VI. V. 3. 71. *v.i.* to assert, warrant.

Vizard, *sb.* mask.

Waft, *v.t.* to beckon. C. of E. II. 2. 108. To turn. W.T. I. 2. 371.

Wag, *v.i.* and *v.t.* to move, stir. R III. III. 5. 7. To go one's way. M.A. V. 1. 16.

Wage, *v.t.* to stake, risk. 1 H IV. 4. 20. *v.i.* to contend. Lear, II. 4. 210. Wage equal = be on an equality with. A. & C. V. 1. 31.

Wanion, *sb.* with a wanion = with a vengeance.

Wanton, *sb.* one brought up in luxury, an effeminate person. John, V. 1. 70. *v.i.* to dally, play. W.T. II. 1. 18.

Wappened, *p.p.* of doubtful meaning, perhaps worn out, stale.

Ward, *sb.* guardianship. A.W. I. 1. 5. Defence. L.L.L. III. 1. 131. Guard in fencing. 1 H IV. II. 4. 198. Prison, custody. 2 H VI. V. 1. 112. Lock, bolt. Tim. III. 3. 38. *v.t.* to guard. R III. V. 3. 254.

Warden-pies, *sb.* pies made with the warden, a large baking pear.

Warrantize, *sb.* security, warranty.

Warrener, *sb.* keeper of a warren, gamekeeper.

Watch, *sb.* a watch candle that marked the hours.

Watch, *v.t.* to tame by keeping from sleep.

Waters, *sb.* for all waters = ready for anything.

Wealsmen, *sb.* statesmen.

Web and pin. *sb.* cataract of the eye.

Weeding, *sb.* weeds.

Weet, *v.t.* to know.

Welkin, *sb.* the blue, the sky. Tw.N. II. 3. 61. *adj.* sky-blue. W.T. I. 2. 136.

Whiffler, *sb.* one who cleared the way for a procession, carrying the whiffle or staff of his office.

Whist, *adj.* still, hushed.

Whittle, *sb.* a clasp-knife.

Whoobub, *sb.* hubbub.

Widowhood, *sb.* rights as a widow.

Wilderness, *sb.* wildness.

Wimpled, *p.p.* blindfolded. (A wimple was a wrap or handkerchief for the neck.)

Winchester goose, *sb.* a venereal swelling in the groin, the brothels of Southwark being in the jurisdiction of the Bishop of Winchester.

Window-bars, *sb.* lattice-like embroidery worn by women across the breast.

Windring, *adj.* winding.

Wink, *sb.* a closing of the eyes, sleep. Tp. II. 1. 281. *v.i.* to close the eyes, be blind, be in the dark. C. of E. III. 2. 58.

Winter-ground, *v.t.* to protect a plant from frost by bedding it with straw.

Wipe, *sb.* a brand, mark of shame.

Wise-woman, *sb.* a witch.

Witch, *sb.* used of a man also; wizard.

Woman, *v.t.* woman me = make me show my woman's feelings.

Woman-tired, *adj.* henpecked.

Wondered, *p.p.* performing wonders.

Wood, *adj.* mad.

Woodman, *sb.* forester, hunter. M.W.W. V. 5. 27. In a bad sense, a wencher. M. for M. IV. 4. 163.

Woollen, to lie in the = either to lie in the blankets, or to be buried in flannel, as the law in Shakespeare's time prescribed.

Word, *sb.* to be at a word = to be as good as one's word.

Word, *v.t.* to represent. Cym. I. 4. 15. To deceive with words. A. & C. V. 2. 191.

World, *sb.* to go to the world = to be married. A woman of the world = a married woman. A world to see = a marvel to behold.

Wrangler, *sb.* an opponent, a tennis term.

Wreak, *sb.* revenge. T.A. IV. 3. 33. *v.t.* to revenge. T.A. IV. 3. 51.

Wreakful, *adj.* revengeful.

Wrest, *sb.* a tuning-key.

Wring, *v.i.* to writhe.

Write, *v.r.* to describe oneself, claim to be. Writ as little beard = claimed as little beard. A.W. II. 3. 62.

Writhled, *adj.* shrivelled up, wrinkled.

Wry, *v.i.* to swerve.

Yare, *adj.* and *adv.* ready, active, nimble.

Yarely, *adv.* readily, briskly.

Yearn, *v.t.* and *v.i.* to grieve.

Yellows, *sb.* jaundice in horses.

Yerk, *v.t.* to lash out at, strike quickly.

Yest, *sb.* froth, foam.

Yesty, *adj.* foamy, frothy.

Younker, *sb.* a stripling, youngster novice.

Yslaked, *p.p.* brought to rest.

Zany, *sb.* a fool, buffoon.

BIBLIOGRAPHY

Ackroyd, Peter, *Shakespeare: The Biography*, Vintage, 2006.

Bloom, Harold, *Shakespeare: The Invention of the Human*, Longman, 2000.

Freeman, Philip, *Julius Caesar*, Simon & Schuster, 2009.

Goldsworthy, Adrian, *Caesar*, Phoenix, 2007.

Halliday, F.E., *A Shakespeare Companion*, Penguin, 1964.

Holden, Anthony, *William Shakespeare: An Illustrated Biography*, Little, Brown, 2002.

Kiernon, Victor, *Shakespeare: Poet and Citizen*, Verso, 1993.

Kott, Jan, *Shakespeare Our Contemporary*, Norton Library, 1965.

Plutarch and Waterfield, Robin, *Roman Lives*, Oxford World's Classics, 2008.

Rowse, A.L., *William Shakespeare: A Biography*, HarperCollins, 1963.